"You really think I'm some sort of daredevil?

Matt slowly walked toward Adrienne in the dimly lit barn.

"Aren't you?" she asked, gazing up at him.

"Life isn't worth living if you go by the rule book all the time."

She shook her head. "We've broken enough rules tonight and taken enough chances to last me a lifetime. I might as well have gone skydiving. Not that I'd *ever* want to do something like that, so don't get any ideas," she added quickly.

Matt laughed. "Okay, we'll hold off on that." His laugh softened into a smile as he reached for her. "This is much safer than skydiving."

Funny, she thought as his mouth sought hers, *it doesn't feel much safer....*

In her own words, veteran Arizona author **Vicki Lewis Thompson** "had a ball creating this book," and hopes everyone has just as much fun reading it. The heroine is a conservative stockbroker; the hero, a daredevil pilot. Their relationship is in trouble from the moment she agrees to get into his plane. "Fly-boys are a special breed. They harbor a daredevil streak that will never die," says Vicki, and she should know. Two of the heroes in her life are pilots—her husband and her son. Does she worry? Yes. Does she try to clip their wings? Never! "You have to love them and let them go."

Books by Vicki Lewis Thompson

HARLEQUIN TEMPTATION
288–FOREVER MINE, VALENTINE
344–YOUR PLACE OR MINE

HARLEQUIN SUPERROMANCE
326–SPARKS
389–CONNECTIONS

It Happened One Weekend

VICKI LEWIS THOMPSON

Harlequin Books

TORONTO • NEW YORK • LONDON
AMSTERDAM • PARIS • SYDNEY • HAMBURG
STOCKHOLM • ATHENS • TOKYO • MILAN

With gratitude for the inspiration provided by my critique group: Dave Eff, Margaret Falk, Regan Forest, Karen Hancock, Donna Lepley, Jim Lewis, Wendy Marcus and Don Valdez

Published December 1991

ISBN 0-373-25474-1

IT HAPPENED ONE WEEKEND

1

ADRIENNE BURNHAM sipped her vodka tonic and prepared to work the room. A malfunctioning icemaker had claimed Beverly, her hostess and friend, leaving Adrienne to plunge in alone. She preferred it that way. Maybe now people wouldn't immediately realize that Beverly had organized the cocktail party for Adrienne's benefit.

She fingered one of the rhinestone buttons on her black rayon jacket. Beverly had approved the suit. Businesslike with a touch of glitz, she'd said, perfect for a stockbroker on the rise in Tucson, Arizona. The only woman stockbroker working at the prestigious firm, C. D. Girard and Sons. Adrienne hoped Beverly was right and that this party would provide the jumpstart she needed.

As she scanned the guests, her gaze swung past a broad-shouldered man with his back to her. Startled, she looked again, this time focusing lower. Sure enough, the seat of his gray slacks was splitting, revealing a slice of red underwear.

Adrienne hesitated, hoping someone else, someone he knew, would notice and tell him. The man laughed and shifted his weight, parting the seam another inch. Adrienne waited, but everyone except her seemed oblivious to the problem. Setting her glass on a bookcase, she crossed the room and laid her hand on his sleeve. "Excuse me," she murmured.

He turned in midsentence and gave her a questioning smile.

Attractive guy, she thought. "Beverly needs you to help her with something in the kitchen," she said.

"Sure." Looking puzzled but willing, he waited for her to lead the way.

"That's okay. I'll follow you."

His eyebrows shot up.

"Trust me."

He shrugged and started for the kitchen with Adrienne following close behind. Very close. Once she'd started this rescue operation, she intended to do it right.

"What's the problem?" he said over his shoulder.

"Icemaker."

"Oh."

When they'd reached the hall, Adrienne lowered her voice. "Don't go into the kitchen. Head for Beverly's bedroom."

He stopped and she almost ran into him. "Look," he said, starting to turn around, "This is flattering, but—"

"Don't stop to argue. It's not what you think."

"Then what is it?"

"I'm not after your body. Your pant seam is splitting down the back."

He whirled, splattering his drink all over both of them. His face and neck turned the color of his underwear as he fingered the seat of his pants and backed against the wall. "It sure as hell is."

"I wouldn't make up something like that." She brushed at the front of her jacket.

"Sorry about the drink," he said, surveying his dampened shirt and her suit. "It was mostly water."

"Any chance you're accident-prone?"

He sighed. "Looks that way, doesn't it? Which way's the bedroom?"

Adrienne nodded toward the open door just beyond where they were standing. "You're almost there."

"Can you . . . can you come with me? I haven't the foggiest idea how I'm going to . . ."

"I guess." She glanced quickly toward the living room. No one seemed to be observing their little tableau. "My purse is in there on the bed and I have an emergency sewing kit in it."

"You're a lifesaver." He edged toward the door and backed into the room.

Adrienne followed and closed the door behind her. "Safe."

The man sighed. "Do you think anybody else noticed?"

"I sort of hoped they would," Adrienne admitted, "so I wouldn't have to tell you. But the rip kept getting wider, and with those red . . ." She paused, feeling her cheeks heat up.

"Dammit! I forgot I put those on. Talk about embarrassing. This has got to be—" he stared at her and began to grin "—the funniest damn thing that's ever happened to me," he said, starting to laugh. "Good old studly Matt Kirkland, standing around the swanky cocktail party with his underwear hanging out."

Adrienne smiled. She didn't often meet men who could poke fun at themselves. "And of course the underwear is red."

"Of course. And some guy couldn't notice and pass me the word. It had to be a good-looking blonde, one I'd probably like to impress." He chuckled and shook his head. "Typical."

"Aha! So you *are* accident-prone," she said, noting his compliment. She liked the hazel depth of his eyes, the crinkles around them when he laughed. He might be thirty, she thought, or thirty-one at most.

"I have a reputation for accidents, I'll admit," he said, "but all my accidents turn out okay, so I don't consider it a flaw."

Cocky, she thought, adding that to her evaluation. "Oh? What's the silver lining in this?"

"I met you. Or I almost have. You haven't told me your name."

"Adrienne Burnham." She thought about mentioning her profession and throwing in a plug for investments as a hedge against financial accidents, but she didn't.

"So *you're* Adrienne."

"What do you mean by that?"

"Um, nothing."

"You've heard something about me?"

"Bev said you were very nice," he said, moving aside some coats and sitting on the bed.

"When?" Adrienne asked, as a horrible suspicion took root.

"She said you were nice all the time."

"No, I mean when was she talking about me?" Adrienne pictured Beverly priming all her guests to be nice to Adrienne, her friend, who needed clients desperately.

"Last week, when she invited me to the party."

Adrienne flushed. "And she told you to buy stocks and bonds from me, if at all possible, because I'm struggling to make it as a broker, right?"

"Wrong."

"Wrong?"

"I didn't know until this minute what you do for a living."

"Oh." She cleared her throat. "Looks like I blew that one. Listen, I'd appreciate it if you'd keep my last confession to yourself. Beverly threw this shindig mostly for me to meet potential clients, because I *am* struggling, but I'd hoped to be somewhat more subtle in my approach."

"No problem. After the way you saved my butt, literally, I can keep a few secrets for you. So how do we fix this little glitch of mine?"

She paused. She hadn't really considered what her offer to sew up his seam would entail. "You'll have to take them off."

He shrugged. "You wouldn't get any surprises. You already know about the red Jockies."

"True." She tried to copy his nonchalance. The situation they found themselves in made false modesty silly, she supposed. She'd certainly seen men in their underwear before. Nevertheless, when he nudged off his shoes and stood up to unbuckle his belt, she walked to the other side of the bed, sat down and made herself very busy finding her purse and digging out the sewing kit. "Speaking of reputations, I hope no one noticed me herding you in here," she said.

His zipper rasped. "If anyone did, I'll happily defend your honor."

She could tell from the rustling and jingle of change that his pants were off. Stupid, but her heart pounded and her mouth was dry. She reminded herself that he had on more clothes than if they'd been at the beach. But they weren't at the beach; they were in a bedroom with the door closed, and her hands shook as she located a needle and thread.

He walked around the bed and handed her his slacks. She glanced up quickly in order to take them. The glance was long enough. His muscular thighs and the red bikini briefs peeked through the dangling tail of his dress shirt exactly at eye level. She swallowed and wondered how she'd ever thread the needle.

"A sewing kit in your purse," he said, sitting next to her on the bed. "I'm impressed. You must be a very organized lady."

"Well, yes . . . I . . ." She struggled with the thread, dampening the end and poking it unsuccessfully at the wavering eye of the needle. "For my work, I . . . need to be . . . organized." She wanted to ask him to move away, but that would only call attention to her awareness of his seminakedness.

"I'll bet you're great at investments. Wish I could be one of your clients, but I just spent all my money on a Cessna. I'm broke."

"That's too bad." Adrienne put the thread in her mouth and tried again.

"No, it's good. I'm starting my own flight school."
He watched for a moment. "Caffeine jitters?"

"I guess," she fibbed.

"That's what you get for drinking too much coffee at
work today. Want me to try to thread it?"

"I'll do it," she said through clenched teeth. By sheer
luck, the thread slipped through the hole. She knotted
it and picked up his slacks. "You're a pilot?" she asked,
vaguely remembering he'd mentioned something about
a plane.

"Yeah. I'm an instructor for light planes. Until now,
I've worked for other people, using rentals. Then along
came this chance to pick up a Cessna for a terrific price.
A great buy, but it wiped out my savings."

Adrienne tried to concentrate on what he was saying. He'd blown all his reserve cash on an airplane. Not
a very sound financial decision. The guy might be
alerting all her hormones, but he wasn't smart with
money, obviously, whereas Alex—she really admired
Alex's ability to parlay his earnings into a sizable nest
egg. Still, Alex's after-shave didn't make her break out
in goose bumps, which was what happened every time
she took a breath sitting next to Matt.

"Adrienne?"

"What?" She jumped and stuck herself with the needle. "Damn." She sucked her bleeding finger.

"A little spaced out, aren't you?"

She took her finger out of her mouth and hoped she
wouldn't bleed on his dove-gray slacks. "Not in the
least."

"Then how come you haven't answered my question?"

"What question?"

"I asked if you'd ever flown in a private plane before. I asked you twice."

"Oh." She turned to him and tried to think of a plausible excuse for having ignored his attempt at conversation. Instead she imagined the silky texture of his hair, the color of Colombian coffee, beneath her fingertips. His mouth had the sculpted precision of a Greek statue, and it curved, ever so slightly, as she continued to stare at him.

"You know," he said, "there seems to be something going on here." His tone indicated amusement as well as a deeper emotion, a mirror image of her own fascination.

"I—I don't know what you're talking about," she stammered. "I—"

Someone rapped on the bedroom door. "Adrienne? You in there?"

She froze. Beverly.

"Adrienne?" Beverly opened the door and stopped, her mouth gaping.

"Matt's pants...uh...broke," Adrienne said, stumbling through her explanation. "I offered to—"

"She rescued me," Matt said. "You were right about her, Bev. She's terrific."

"Adrienne *is* terrific," Beverly agreed, recovering herself with a chuckle. "And I'm glad you two are getting to know each other. I'm sorry to interrupt the *mending* session, but your roommate's on the phone, Adrienne. She sounded urgent about something." Beverly nodded toward the telephone on the bedside table. "You can take it in here." Then she quietly closed the door.

Adrienne turned to Matt. "Beverly wanted to set us up, didn't she? That's what all the stuff about me being very nice was all about. She's matchmaking!"

Matt smiled. "Better take your call."

"But she didn't even warn me. She's supposed to be my friend, and she didn't—"

"Bev said it was urgent," he reminded her.

"You're right. We'll work this out later." Adrienne put down his slacks and picked up the receiver of the phone next to her. "Margaret?"

"Adrienne, I'm sorry. Your mother just called with some bad news."

Adrienne clutched the receiver with both hands. "Dad?" she whispered.

"No, not your dad. Granny. She's very sick, mostly from old age, they said. They're not sure she'll make it through the night. They thought you'd want to know."

"Oh, God." A lump clogged Adrienne's throat. "I'll have to try to get there." A picture of Granny, whinnying at the gate, eager to greet her each day after school, ready for their daily ride, brought blinding tears to her eyes. "I have to see her before . . ."

"Your mom said you'd probably want to come, but they know how hard it'll be to get flights at this hour. You're to call her if you manage to make arrangements," Margaret said. "Is there anything I can do?"

"I don't think so," Adrienne managed to say, sniffing. "I'll handle it from here." She swallowed. "If I can get a flight, I'll go straight to the airport from here.

There's stuff at my parents' home I can wear. So if you don't see me in an hour, expect me back Sunday night."

"Right. I'm sorry, babe."

"I shouldn't be such a wimp, I suppose, but she means so much to me. I thought . . . I thought she'd go on forever."

"Yeah, I know. Be tough."

"I will, Margaret. Goodbye." Adrienne hung up the phone and tried to get a grip on her emotions.

Matt's voice came as a surprise. She'd nearly forgotten about him. "What is it?" he asked gently.

"Granny's dying."

"Hey, that's rough. Where is she?"

"At my parents' home, in Utah. A little town north of Salt Lake City, one you probably haven't heard of. Anyway, I have to go there. Somehow. If I can get a flight to Salt Lake, then I'll rent a car, and—"

"Is there an airstrip nearby?"

She turned on the bed and wiped her eyes. "Near the town?"

"Yes. It can be anything, just for crop dusters, or other light planes."

"You'd take me there?"

"Is my underwear red?"

Adrienne's smile wobbled. "That's a very generous offer."

"I'm a generous guy."

"But I really can't accept. Thanks anyway, though. It's nice of you."

"I can get you there faster than a commercial flight, especially if you have to rent a car to drive from Salt Lake City."

"But you're..." She hesitated. "You said yourself that you're accident-prone. I don't think I can—"

"Hey." He reached for her hand. "I'm a damned good pilot," he said, squeezing her hand, then releasing it. "Ask Bev about me."

Her hand tingled. Her brain tingled. How could such a logical solution appear reckless? Yet it did. Adrienne thought of Granny. Time was everything, and Matt was offering her a savings in time. "If I accepted, I'd pay you for the gas, or fuel, or whatever you use," she said.

He regarded her calmly. "If you insist."

"Look, please don't take this wrong, but I would like to talk to Bev first."

"Sure."

Adrienne stood. "I'll be right back."

"But—"

"I'll fix your pants. Don't worry." Adrienne left the room before he could protest further. She didn't want him with her when she questioned Beverly, and keeping him pantsless was the perfect solution. She found Beverly arranging an assortment of cheese and crackers on a plate.

Beverly glanced up. "Problems?"

"My horse, the one I rode all through 4-H, is dying."

"Oh, dear." Beverly stopped what she was doing and turned to her. "I remember you talking about that horse."

"She's like a member of my family. This may sound stupid, but I'm going there."

"Now?"

"Yes, and Matt's offered to fly me."

"Wow. That's great." Beverly's eyes sparkled. "I was sort of hoping—"

"Never mind that now, Beverly. When I get back I'll discuss this matchmaking stuff you've taken on, but at the moment I need to know if he's a good pilot."

"He's an instructor, Adrienne. They don't let you do that if you're not any good."

"Yeah, I guess, but I just wanted to know if you— would you fly with him?"

Beverly grasped Adrienne's arms and gazed into her face. "Absolutely. In high school, all the girls went crazy over Matt because he took such good care of them. I have no doubt he'd take good care of you. In fact, that's why I—"

"Forget that part, Beverly. All I needed was some re-assurance that I wasn't taking off with some weirdo. After all, so far since I've known him he's split the seat of his pants and spilled a drink on me. I'd hate that to be the beginning of a pattern."

Beverly laughed. "Matt's always getting into little scrapes like that, but never anything very serious. And when the chips are down, you can always count on him. Always."

Adrienne took a deep breath. "Okay, I'll take him up on the offer."

"Good."

"And lose the satisfied smile, Beverly. I'm only do-ing this for Granny's sake. Matt's not my type."

"If you say so."

"I do." Adrienne turned and left the kitchen to cur-tail the possibility of further comments from Beverly. When she opened the bedroom door, she found Matt engrossed in sewing his pants. As she walked in, he glanced up and promptly stabbed himself with the needle.

"Damn!" He sucked on his finger.

"Didn't you think I'd come back and finish the job?"

He took his finger out of his mouth. "Sure, but it wasn't much fun sitting here helplessly waiting for you. I'm a man of action."

Adrienne smiled. "Well, a man of action. I'd like to accept your generous offer to fly me to Utah. And thanks."

"Bev gave me a good recommendation?"

"Sterling."

"Good old Bev." He held up his slacks. "In that case, I'd better get you to finish this up right. I fly by the seat of my pants."

"You do what?"

"Just kidding."

"Listen, Matt, maybe we'd better forget this whole—"

"It was just a little joke, Burnham!" he said, waving both hands. "Boy, are you cautious."

"Please don't joke about flying, okay?"

"Okay." He handed her the slacks and she sat down beside him to finish sewing them up. "You haven't ever been in a single-engine plane, have you?" he asked.

"No."

"Are you afraid?"

Adrienne thought about Granny, of the soft trust in her warm brown eyes. "Of course not," she said, sewing the last few stitches and handing the slacks to Matt.

"While you put these on, I'll call my folks and tell them what we plan to do."

"Okay. And don't worry. Everything will work out fine."

"I have no doubt it will," Adrienne lied. She reached for the phone and turned away so she couldn't see the provocative picture he made as he got dressed.

MATT PARKED his aging Corvette on the tarmac of the small, privately owned airport where he kept his plane. As Adrienne got out of the car and walked toward the orange-and-white Cessna, her straight, jaw-length hair blew around her face. She glanced up, but no clouds marred the star-studded sky. "What about the weather?"

"I checked. Should be okay."

Adrienne studied the plane that would carry her up into the blackness. It had a single propeller and the wings were attached above the doors. "This isn't very big, is it?"

"It's a four-passenger. Biggest one I could afford," Matt said, unhooking the tie-downs from one wing. "Can you get the other side?"

"Um, sure." Rounding the plane, she tucked her purse under her arm and wrestled with the hook. When it came loose, it broke one of her carefully tended fingernails, and she swore softly.

"Okay?" he asked from the tail section.

"Yeah." The fingernail would grow again. It was the thought of losing Granny she found unbearable.

Matt came up beside her and unlocked the passenger door. "Climb in and we'll get this baby airborne," he said, holding the door open.

Adrienne gauged the height of the step positioned on the stationary landing gear and considered how far her narrow skirt would stretch without ripping. Fortunately no one but Matt was around. "There's only one way to do this," she said, hiking her skirt up to mid-thigh.

"No complaints from me," he said, helping her up.

"A gentleman wouldn't look."

"Who says I did?"

She glanced down at him and evaluated his grin. He'd looked, all right. "Shall we go?"

"Yep." He closed her door and walked around to his side of the plane.

"Does anybody have to push that propeller around for us?" she asked as he latched his door and picked up the headset.

"This sweetheart is old, but not that old."

"How old?" Adrienne's stomach became queasy.

"Never mind." He hung the headset around his neck and patted her hand, which was, she noticed, clutching her purse as if it were a parachute rip cord. "You can throw your purse in the back seat."

"Why?"

"So you'll have both hands free in case..." He reached into his sportcoat pocket and pulled out a paper bag. "Got this from Beverly before we left. Considering you're a first-timer."

"Oh." Adrienne followed his instructions and tossed her purse onto the back seat.

"In fact, I usually put my wallet back there," he said, easing up from the seat to extract it from his back pocket. "When I'm driving or flying, I hate having that thing pressing into me."

"Tender bottom?" she teased without thinking. Nerves, she thought, gave her loose lips.

"Right," he said, glancing at her with amusement. Then he reached for the ignition. "Want earplugs?"

Adrienne shook her head. She wanted to be able to hear every little throb of that engine.

The Cessna kicked over with a reassuring roar, although the plane vibrated more than Adrienne would have liked. Matt revved the engine and consulted the bank of dials in front of him.

"Is something wrong?" she shouted.

"Nope."

"Why aren't we moving?"

"I'm preflighting the plane."

"Oh." Adrienne didn't know what that meant, but she'd assume it meant something good. At last the plane began rolling slowly forward, moving from the tie-down area to the runway. Adrienne's heart beat faster. As they taxied past the white lights lining the runway, she tried breathing the way she'd been taught in aerobics class—in through the nose, out through the mouth. She could do this. Granny was worth it.

The radio crackled as Matt talked with someone in the control tower. He veered the plane in a half circle, faced it into the wind, and paused.

She looked at him, silently questioning.

"We're fine," he said gently. "We're cleared for take-off. Don't look so scared." He started to say something else, but instead he shook his head, leaned over and kissed her soundly on the mouth.

"What was that for?" she said, gasping.

"To give you something else to think about. Hang on."

2

THE TINY PLANE barreled down the runway, shaking as if every rivet would pop loose before they became airborne. Adrienne gripped the seat, but her overwhelming anxiety had been displaced with another emotion. He'd kissed her. With no warning, he'd just up and kissed her. The only male who'd ever tried that had been Kenny Christopherson in second grade, and she'd knocked him off the monkey bars for his insolence. Nowadays, men, including Alex, told her she was intimidating. Apparently Matt Kirkland wasn't particularly intimidated.

She moistened her lips. The kiss had felt pretty good, but so what? It was the only one they'd ever share. This cocky pilot who'd sunk all his savings into a rattletrap plane certainly wasn't the type for her, no matter what ideas to the contrary he might have. Maybe he thought, because he'd offered to take her to Utah, that she'd be so grateful that she'd—well, he could think again.

She became aware that he was smiling at her . . . and that they were off the ground. The lights of the airport grew smaller, surrounded by darkness, but off on the horizon Tucson glittered like a velvet-lined jewelry box displaying its gems.

"Not so bad, huh?" he said over the drone of the engine.

She glanced at him, not knowing if he could hear her with the headset on. "Is that how you calm all your passengers?" she shouted.

He laughed. "First tell me if it worked."

She answered him with her best glare.

"I'll take that as a 'yes.'" With a self-satisfied smile, he returned his attention to the control panel.

Her stomach flipped again, but not from fear. Matt affected her in ways that safe, responsible Alex never had. Alex. She hadn't thought to call him and tell him she was leaving. Maybe Beverly or Margaret would, but on second thought probably not. Neither of them thought much of Alex. Beverly had told Adrienne not to bring him to the cocktail party. Her excuse was that Adrienne didn't need competition from another stockbroker, and a man, at that, when the party was designed to bring her clients. Adrienne now suspected Beverly's motives were a bit more complicated.

Anyway, Adrienne had completely forgotten about Alex in the confusion of taking this flight to see Granny. She'd call him when she reached Utah. He'd understand. Of course he would. She could stop feeling guilty any time now. Except that when she looked at Matt her emotions pirouetted wildly; this brought on a fresh surge of guilt because she hadn't been able to muster half as much excitement for Alex.

Of course, technically she was a free woman. She wasn't engaged to Alex and hadn't even slept with him. Still, he'd waited patiently in hopes that soon, when she felt ready, they would . . . Last weekend he'd mentioned that after three months he thought her reluctance a little silly. She'd used the same argument she'd always used. With both her older sisters divorced, Adrienne planned to be the exception. She'd marry and stay married. Her formula for success included caution at the outset of a relationship and a long, careful courtship. Many women she knew, including her sisters, allowed sexual attraction to lead them into unsuitable matches. She was determined not to repeat their mistakes.

"See there?" Matt's voice made her jump. "Nothing to it," he said, sliding the headset from his ears and hanging it around his neck.

"Shouldn't you put that back on?" she asked.

"I can hear okay, if anything comes up."

Far on the horizon a flash of lightning stretched downward, followed by a roll of thunder a few seconds later.

"A storm!" Adrienne cried, leaning forward and peering out. "A storm's out there."

"Does look like it." Matt replaced the headset. "Sometimes they blow in unexpectedly." He spoke into his mouthpiece, communicating with control tower personnel somewhere below them.

Adrienne watched a second lightning bolt and counted the seconds until the thunder. The storm marched closer.

Matt removed his headset again. "Sure enough, a little squall isn't behaving as expected," he said evenly.

"But what will we do?"

"Keep tabs on it. Go around it if necessary."

"Go around?"

"Sure. No problem."

"Are you telling me everything?"

He glanced at her and smiled. "What would you like to know?"

She returned his smile and mimicked his casual attitude. "I want to know if we're going to crash and die."

"Thanks for the vote of confidence. The answer is no."

She felt chastised. After his generous offer of this flight he didn't deserve sarcasm. "I'm sorry."

"You are afraid, aren't you?"

"It's . . . unfamiliar." Adrienne shuddered as lightning connected two thunderheads, illuminating them from within like giant electric bulbs.

"Want me to quote you some statistics?" Matt offered. "More people die in cars than in light planes. You're safer than you would have been driving a rental car to your parents' house."

"I've heard that one."

"You don't believe it."

"I believe it. But up here, with the sky full of thousands of volts of electricity, and the ground very far away, and no parachutes or anything, statistics are cold comfort."

He glanced at her. "Guess it's time for more distractions."

"Don't you dare take your hands off those controls!"

"Easy does it," he said. "I didn't mean that kind. Let's try conversation. Do you have a boyfriend?"

She hesitated.

"Come on, Adrienne. I can't talk stocks and bonds, and obviously you can't swap flying stories, so boyfriends and girlfriends are a good, juicy topic."

"That's your opinion."

Matt laughed. "Boyfriends aren't a juicy topic with you? I'm surprised. I'd have thought you'd have to beat them off with a stick. I think you're holding out on me. Whose heart are you breaking this week?"

"I really don't think it's **any** of your business."

He laughed again. "Okay. I'll go first. Let's see. My first love was Tina. We were five, and played doctor all the time, until Tina's mother ruined the game. Then I went through that male bonding phase when all the guys hate all the girls, but when I was twelve, I met this older woman of sixteen, and she—"

"I really don't want to hear this, Matt."

"Too tame for you? Okay, I'll cut to the chase. My most passionate, long-lasting affair was with a dynamite girl I met in college. No inhibitions whatsoever. That woman would do it anywhere—in the bathtub, in a hot air balloon, on a bicycle—"

"A bicycle?"

"Yeah. Of course, I'd have to peddle, and it was a little hard to steer with—"

"Stop." Adrienne flushed and looked out at the rolling dark clouds.

"You don't want to hear about it?"

"No." She clenched her jaw and tried to calm the riotous, sensual feelings he'd generated. "I think it's very inappropriate for you to be revealing the details of your sex life. I hardly know you. Furthermore, how would this woman react if she knew that you were using her as a topic of conversation?"

He gave a sly grin. "You're assuming something."

"I'm assuming that you're an arrogant braggart who thinks nothing of boasting about the most intimate details of his private life to a stranger."

"You're also assuming that I'm telling you the truth. The fact is, I'm a terrific storyteller."

She eyed him warily. "You . . . made that up?"

"Not all. The parts about Tina and the sixteen-year-old are true." He chuckled. "But I think you'd kill yourself making love on a bicycle."

Adrienne gasped. "You lied?"

"I created an entertaining fiction. Admit it. I had you going there for a while."

That's an understatement, she thought. She couldn't let him know how he affected her. A guy like Matt would jump right in and take advantage of the situation. He might have made up the story about the bicycle, but she'd bet money he'd participated in his share of real-life sexual exploits. The red underwear gave her a clue, and she could imagine the rest—a very good-looking single man, with a manner about him that encouraged . . . well, she wouldn't allow that sort of looseness in her thinking.

Lightning split the sky, seeming near enough to touch, and she jerked in surprise. He'd made her forget. He'd distracted her, just as he'd promised. For the length of time he'd roped her into thinking about his sex life, she'd been too busy to be afraid. Reluctantly she acknowledged the effectiveness of his methods, but she wished he didn't always have to appeal to her libido. Her reactions were becoming disturbingly predictable.

"Your turn," he said, guiding the plane easily through the darkness. "Who's Alex?"

"So you know about him, too. Did Beverly hand you my résumé?"

"Don't get defensive. She merely said you were dating a boring guy named Alex and she'd love to see you explore your options a little more."

Adrienne pressed her lips together. "When I get back to Tucson, I'll have a little talk with Beverly. Boosting my career is one thing, but meddling in my social life is a whole different kettle of fish."

"Hey, you know Bev. She means well."

"Speaking of which, how well do you know her? She mentioned something about high school when I asked about you tonight. Was that in Tucson?"

"Yeah. I was an Air Force brat and my dad was stationed here. We left my senior year, but I always wanted to come back. Besides, it's a heck of a place to fly. I moved back a few months ago, and ran into Bev last week in the grocery store."

"And she invited you to come to the party and meet me," Adrienne finished.

He glanced at her. "Yep. She thought we might get along."

Adrienne met his gaze, but she could find nothing to say that wouldn't bring her more trouble than she already had. A few raindrops spattered the windshield. "Where are we?"

"North of Phoenix."

"How far from Flagstaff?"

"A good hundred miles. We're over the mesa country, and soon we'll—damn."

"Damn?" She peered at him.

He didn't answer and replaced the headset.

"Matt, what is it?" In a moment her question was answered; even to her untutored ear, the engine sounded funny, like someone with a bad cold. She knew from Matt's grim manner as he worked with the controls that something was very wrong.

He spoke tersely into the headset, but all she could hear were crackles and hisses in return. He mumbled something that sounded like "damned interference." The engine continued to cough and sputter. Then he gave her a brief glance. "We're landing."

"Landing?" Her heart thumped rapidly. "Where? Is there an airport?"

He shook his head. "Maybe I can find a space on the highway."

"The highway?" Panic gripped her with icy fingers. "Matt, you can't land out in the middle of the highway!"

"You may be right." He banked the plane and looked out the window through wisps of rain-laden fog. Then he muttered an oath.

"What? What's wrong?"

"The traffic is spaced out, but steady. Not enough room. I could cause a wreck down there."

"Then what will we do?"

"Find a clear space."

"In the middle of nowhere?"

"I have no choice, okay?" he said through his teeth. "Now shut up and do as I tell you."

She couldn't breathe. "Matt," she choked. "Are we going to crash?"

"Not if I can help it."

"Oh, God." Adrienne shut her eyes. "Oh, God," she whispered again. She thought of her mother, so concerned on the phone. Tears burned her eyes. Why had she agreed to this stupid idea? If only she could go back to that moment in Beverly's bedroom and say, as she should have said, "No, I'll take a commercial flight." What a fool she was. And now...

The plane's engine coughed itself into terrifying silence as they began a steep descent. Adrienne swallowed rapidly. She wouldn't throw up. She wouldn't.

"Lean over as far as you can and tuck your head between your legs," Matt said, his words a cold command.

Adrienne did her best, considering her skirt, and the shaking she couldn't control. If she lived through this, she would never act on impulse again. Never.

"Hang on. Here we go."

The jolt threw her against her seat belt, and bile rose in her throat. She swallowed it back as the plane careened up on one wheel and smashed back to the ground. The impact brought her teeth together with a snap, catching the side of her tongue. She tasted blood.

Beside her Matt swore in a continuous stream as the plane bucked across the rocky, uneven landscape. "Stop, damn you, stop!" he shouted.

Gradually the plane slowed, and Adrienne realized they weren't going to die. Not yet, anyway. Ahead of them lay more rocky terrain, and beyond that...black nothingness.

"What's that?" she asked in a hoarse whisper. "A lake?"

"No. Unfasten your seat belt in case we have to jump. And pray that this baby stops before we get to that point."

Adrienne prayed. The void loomed closer. They'd go over the edge. They'd—

The plane stopped. All she could see ahead was blackness.

"We must be right on the rim," Matt said in a monotone, as if any inflection might tip the balance and send them over. "Open your door very carefully. I'll sit here until you're out."

"But—"

"Don't argue with me. Do it."

She wondered if she could. Her hand fumbled with the latch.

"Easy, Burnham. Easy. Like a cat."

Like a cat, she thought. Right. Any minute they could plunge into infinity, cartwheeling down the canyon to die in a ball of flame. Cats had nine lives. Jellyfish had only one.

Somehow she got the door open. She pushed it gently, not even breathing. The plane rocked and she cried out. Then it settled again. She tried not to think about the chasm, or what would happen if her movements saved her but sacrificed Matt. "You go, too," she whispered.

"Not until you're out."

"We could jump together."

"Get the hell out of this plane, Adrienne. Now!"

She swallowed. "Okay." Biting down hard on her back teeth, she eased out of her seat. The plane groaned but didn't move. She put her foot on the metal step just as lightning streaked across the sky and revealed the gaping canyon in front of them in frightening detail, a monster's mouth that made her stomach clutch. She gasped out Matt's name.

"Go."

Taking a deep breath, she put her weight on the step and moved the other foot down to the plane's wheel cover. The plane trembled.

"That's it," Matt encouraged. "Just climb down."

Thunder rumbled overhead. She paused, wanting to separate out the noises of the plane. It creaked but seemed steady.

"Once you're out, I'll make a dive for it," Matt said. "So get away from the fuselage, in case it pitches around."

"I will." Her heartbeat hammered in her ears, eliminating her chances of listening for telltale creaking from the plane. She had to go, had to believe that Matt would make it, too. She kept her eyes on her feet. The wheel cover was about a yard from the precipice, but the nose and propeller hung over the edge. "Okay," she called. "I'm putting my foot on the ground. Get out, Matt."

"Put your other foot down and get away."

"I'm down, Matt," she called as a gust of wind pushed at the plane. She stumbled across the uneven brush-covered ground as he'd instructed. Her heel caught in the rocks and she pitched forward, scraping her hands and knees as she broke her fall.

Behind her, Matt yelled. She rolled over and sat up in time to watch the plane, groaning and screeching, nose-dive into the canyon. She should have disobeyed him, held on to the tail. Her throat opened but no sound came out. Roaring filled her ears, deafening her to the sound of the crash. Then there was silence, except for her pounding heart. "Matt?" His name was only a whisper.

The lightning flickered again and she strained to see. *There he was.* Thank God, he was lying several yards from her, where he'd hurled himself as the plane had begun its slide. With a cry of relief she scrambled to her feet and raced toward him.

He sat up and gazed in bewilderment at the spot where the plane had been. Then he looked at Adrienne, as if he was wondering who she was. "It's gone," he said, sounding confused.

"But you're not." She dropped to her knees and flinched at the pain. "You're alive, Matt. We're both alive. We made it."

"My plane's gone," he said again in that same disbelieving tone.

"Planes can be replaced," she said, catching his face between her hands. "People can't. Matt, you almost died saving me. You were—" Tears trickled down her cheeks as reaction set in. "You were wonderful. I can't tell you how—"

"Don't cry," he said, looking as if he might, too.

"But we almost died. And you made me go first. You d-don't even know me, and you were so b-brave." She began to sob.

"Don't cry," he said again, and gathered her in his arms.

Tension flooded out of her in great, choking gasps. He stroked her hair and murmured softly. Finally her outburst subsided, but she kept her face buried against the comforting bulk of his shoulder. "I . . . need something to blow my nose on," she mumbled, sniffing.

He moved just enough to dig in his back pocket and produce a handkerchief, which he placed in her hand.

"Thanks." She sat back and blew her nose. Then she looked at him. "Well, what now?"

As if in answer, the skies opened up and rain pelted down on them.

Matt gave her a faint smile. "You had to ask, didn't you?"

"Don't look at me. I'm not the one with a reputation for being accident-prone."

He sobered. "Look, Adrienne, don't start."

"I'm sorry," she said, instantly contrite. He'd lost his plane, his most cherished possession, and almost lost his life trying to save her. "Do you . . . do you think it's done for?"

"Good question." He heaved himself to his feet. "Maybe I can see something down there."

"Matt," she said, scrambling up and following him. "Don't get too close to the edge."

He ignored her warning. "I don't remember hearing an explosion," he said, moving out onto a ledge hanging over the canyon. A scraggly juniper clung to the lip of the precipice.

"Matt, please be careful." She hung back. The only way she'd be able to reach the edge was on her hands and knees, and even the thought of doing that made her stomach jump. How she'd ever made it out of the plane while it perched on the brink of the canyon, she'd never know. She couldn't even look out the windows of sky-scrapers without feeling dizzy.

"I can't see it," Matt said. "In the dark, with this rain, I can't tell where it landed. But there's no fire. That's a good sign."

"If you can't see it, why don't you come back over here and get away from the edge."

He glanced at her. "You're afraid of heights, aren't you?"

"A little," she hedged. "Please come back over here, Matt."

He took one last look into the canyon. "Might as well. Can't see a blasted thing down there. But if there wasn't a fire, maybe the plane can be salvaged, or at least parts of it. Maybe I won't lose everything," he said, walking back through the rain toward her.

"What about insurance?"

"You mean airframe insurance?"

"Whatever you call it. Coverage to replace the plane."

"There isn't any."

"What? Aren't you required to have it?"

"Not if I own the plane outright, which I do, or what's left of it. I have to carry liability on passengers, but I couldn't afford the other stuff right now."

Adrienne's shoulders slumped. "I can't believe this. You put all your savings into a plane and didn't buy insurance?"

"I meant to, as soon as I scraped together the extra cash."

"Matt, that's terrible financial planning. You don't leave your chief financial asset unprotected. You—"

"Look, Burnham," he said, striding forward and pointing a finger in her face. "Save that for your clients, okay? I feel bad enough about losing my plane. I don't need some lecture on fiscal responsibility, in the middle of the night, in the pouring rain, from a woman I was trying—in my own misguided way—to help."

"I was only—"

"Can it!"

"All right," she said quietly. "I'll can it, but I do have one teeny-weeny question."

"What?"

"What the hell are we going to do now?"

"We wait."

"We do *what?*"

"Stay with the wreckage."

"You forgot something," she said, as rain streamed down her face. "We can't get *to* the wreckage. Maybe nobody can. Maybe nobody will be able to see it, even in daylight. Maybe it's in a million pieces!"

He winced. "It's not."

"How do you know?"

"I can feel it."

Adrienne threw up her hands. "Oh. I'd forgotten the male habit of bonding with machines. Well, you may *feel* that staying with your plane is essential, but I don't. I'm hiking until I find a road."

"That's dumb, Adrienne. All our cash and ID's are down there with the plane and we're dressed in party clothes. Even if you found a road, who would pick up a bedraggled woman, with dripping hair, scraped knees, a ripped skirt—"

"It's ripped?" Adrienne looked down at herself and noticed the jagged tear up the left side that exposed most of her thigh. She grabbed the material and pulled it together.

Matt laughed. "Hey, I think we're beyond modesty, Burnham. No matter what we do, our clothes keep coming apart on us. And if you're worried that I might get all hot and bothered and ravish you in the mud and rocks, you're overestimating either your appeal or my sex drive."

She glared at him. "You're impossible."

"Gee, and only a little while ago you were telling me I'm wonderful. What happened?"

She stood there, her three-inch heels sinking slowly into the mud, her rayon suit and good nylons ruined, her hair running with water, her mascara stinging her eyes. In a few hours her parents would be hysterical with worry, and chances were she'd never make it home in time to see Granny alive. "I guess maybe I'm not at my best under these conditions," she said, turning away and slopping through the mud.

"Where are you going?"

"To find a road."

"Adrienne, be reasonable."

She turned back to him. "You mean, see it your way. You want to stay and watch over your precious plane, but I'm thinking of my parents, who in a few hours will be out of their minds with worry. If we reach a highway, we can have someone take us to a telephone."

"*If* we reach a highway."

"I meant to say *when*. Now, I'm going, whether you want to come with me or not." She turned and started off, grimacing at the pain in her knees and the sharp bite of the rocks through the thin soles of her shoes.

"I should just let you go!" he called after her. "If you want to be independent, I should just let you be independent!"

She kept on walking and didn't answer. She'd like to have him along, but if he chose not to come with her, she'd find the road by herself. There had to be one out there. This country wasn't that desolate. Not long ago they'd flown over a highway. She'd head in the direction from which they'd come.

She strained to hear the sound of his footsteps, but heard only her own. Her foot slipped in the mud. She tried to steady herself on a nearby bush and grabbed a handful of thorns. "Damn"! she cried, stopping to peer at her hand. "This is unfriendly country."

Fortunately she hadn't grabbed cactus, and the thorns pulled easily out of her skin. Still, she had fresh marks on her palm next to the scrapes on the heel of her hand. She held out her hand to the rain, figuring she'd better wash the area, much as it hurt to do so. Then she began trudging forward again, trying to watch where she stepped.

Finding a path through the prickly underbrush wasn't a simple job. If she chose to walk on bare ground, she sank in mud, but her smooth leather soles slid on the rocks. She kept her head down most of the time, to watch where she was going and to shield her face from the pelting rain.

Suddenly some sixth sense warned her to glance up, and as she did, she let out a piercing shriek. Directly in front of her loomed a dark, forbidding figure.

3

"YOU'RE GOING in the wrong direction, Adrienne," the threatening figure said in Matt's voice.

Relief was followed swiftly by anger. "How dare you frighten me like that?"

"If I'd followed behind, like a good boy, and called out, would you have stopped to listen?" He stepped closer. Rain soaked his sport coat and plastered his hair to his head.

"Maybe I wouldn't have stopped right away, but you didn't have to scare me to death to get my attention."

"What would you suggest? That I should have grabbed you? You'd probably have decked me."

"I would not have! I—"

"Anyway, forget about that," he said with a wave of his arm. "If you're trying to find a road, you'd better go that way," he said, pointing to the right.

Her fury returned. "You *knew* where the road was. You knew all along and wouldn't tell me."

"I knew the *direction* of the road," he said, his tone hard. "God knows what lies between here and there, and how long we'll have to hike to find the road. Then probably nobody will come along, and if they do, they'd have to be fools to pick up a pair like us."

"Did you say 'we'?"

He sighed. "Yeah."

"You're coming with me?"

"I have no choice. The way you're going, you'll fall down the other side of the mesa."

"I was only going back the way we came," she said, sticking out her chin.

"Afraid not."

"I was, too."

"If you believe that, you have a lousy sense of direction, which means I really can't leave you out here to wander around. People with no sense of direction go in circles until they drop."

"So what do you care?" Tears of frustration joined the rain sliding down her cheeks.

"Sometimes I ask myself the same question." He gazed at her through the rain. "Let's go." He turned and trudged off in the direction he'd indicated before.

She struggled after him. A helping hand now and then would have been nice, but pride kept her from asking. He thought he was so smart, this pilot who hadn't even bothered to take out insurance. She still couldn't believe it. Served him right to lose the plane.

"There's a wash up ahead," he called over his shoulder. "Looks like it's running."

"Any way around it?" Adrienne doubted her ability to wade through a running stream, considering how much trouble her high heels were giving her on relatively solid ground.

"Who can tell in this downpour?"

She tottered up beside him. The water churned below, shallow but nasty-looking, with rocks and branches creating miniature rapids. The view up the wash, what little she could see, promised no better, and downstream appeared deeper yet. She'd be a mass of cuts and bruises by the time she clambered across this barrier, but she'd have to try. "Let's go," she said, starting down the bank.

"Wait." He grabbed her arm. "I'll carry you."

"That's not necessary," she said in her haughtiest manner.

He muttered an earthy expression.

"Profanity isn't going to—" She gasped as he tightened his grip on her arm, and without further discussion, heaved her headfirst over his shoulder. "Matt, stop this nonsense! I can get across myself."

"Sure you can," he said, grunting with the effort of lugging her down the embankment. "But I have to prove my manliness."

"Exactly!" Her ears buzzed as blood rushed to her head. Upside-down wasn't her favorite position and she was getting dizzy. "That's my whole point," she shouted above the noise of the water surging around his knees. "This male urge of yours to take charge. You—"

"Shut up, Adrienne." He was breathing hard, but he managed a chuckle. "God, you're something. Here you are, ass in the air, debating sexual politics."

"I'll thank you not to refer to my anatomy in such a coarse way, Mr. Kirkland."

He chuckled again.

"What was that for?"

"Can't tell you," he said, patting her bottom, "without referring to your anatomy."

"How dare you!" she cried, intensely aware of her skirt bunched at her hips, her legs bare except for the remaining shreds of her stockings, and Matt's firm grip on her thighs.

"Stop squirming," he said, shifting her weight so his cheek rested against her hip, "or we'll both go in the drink."

"I think you're *enjoying* this."

"Not so's you'd notice, but I take my fun where I can."

"Matt Kirkland, I demand that you—"

"Oopsy-daisy," he said, and set her upright at the edge of the water on the other side of the stream.

Avoiding his gaze, she leaned down and tugged at the hem of her tattered skirt. Neither the skirt nor her dignity would ever be the same. There was also the problem of his touch, still imprinted on her skin. "I think maybe the rain's stopping," she said.

"Maybe."

She glanced up at his tone.

He watched her with arms folded. "Tell me, Adrienne, does there ever come a time when you say to hell with it and just let loose?"

She straightened and glared at him. "If I ever did, it wouldn't be with you."

"*If* you ever did? You mean, you never have?"

"That's none of your business."

"You're missing out, Burnham. Life's to be lived, not avoided. It's full of a million little sinful pleasures."

"You mean, like this?" She held out her arms. "Flying off into the night in a defective plane, during a thunderstorm, with no insurance, dressed in what used to be our best clothes?"

Matt grinned. "You have to admit, you're not bored."

"How can you make jokes?"

"How can you be serious?" He laughed and shook his head. "Come here."

"Wha—" Before she realized what he was doing, she found herself pulled into his arms, her protests silenced with a rain-drenched kiss. Then he lifted his head and smiled at her. "Just checking."

For a moment she couldn't react. The kiss was so unexpected and...warm. Then she recovered herself and pushed him away. "What do you mean 'just checking'?" she asked, mustering as much indignation as she could, considering the feelings swirling through her. Obviously when it came to sinful pleasures, Matt knew the territory.

"Checking to see if I'd imagined something before takeoff," he said. "But I was right."

"Right?"

"Your kiss is a hell of a lot sweeter than what comes out of your mouth."

She clenched both hands and longed to hit him. But she considered herself too much of a lady for that. "I'll thank you to keep your judgments to yourself," she said. "Not to mention your damned kisses."

"My, my. Such bitterness. Is it just me, or do you react this way to all men?"

Adrienne sighed. "This is neither the time nor the place to discuss—"

"You can make it brief. Just satisfy my curiosity."

"All right, you asked for it. I don't react negatively to all men, just your type."

"My type? And what's that?"

"The type who craves the glamour of his own plane, but doesn't bother with mundane things like insurance. The type who has to have a sports car, who assumes he knows what's best, who flings women over his shoulder despite their protests, and thinks he can solve every problem with sex."

"Sex? How did sex get into this?"

"You kissed me! Twice!"

Matt laughed. "Lady, if that qualifies as sex in your mind, you've been seriously deprived by this Alex character."

"That's exactly what I mean," she retorted, resisting the excitement his words engendered. "Besides being impulsive and irresponsible, you're infuriatingly cocky."

He gazed at her. "You're right about the insurance. I was crazy not to get it, even if I had to borrow the money."

His admission caught her off guard and she faltered. "That's—that's right," she stammered. "You should have borrowed if necessary." Darn him, he wasn't reacting predictably. Just when she'd made a solid case against him, he threw her off guard by agreeing with her.

"As for impulsive, I guess I am. And as for cocky—" He paused and his gaze swept over her. "You'd have to know a lot more about me to make that assessment. Maybe I'm just confident."

"Hah." She tingled all over. "I don't need to know more about you. Nor do I want to."

His slow smile challenged her statement.

"There, see what I mean?" she said. "Cocky."

"No," he said softly.

She stared at him as dangerous urges coursed through her. She tightened all her muscles against the pull of his sensuality and vowed not to succumb to it. "Let's find that road," she said.

He held out his hand. Ignoring it, she turned away and climbed the embankment alone.

They hiked in silence. Rain pattered intermittently around them, but the worst of the deluge seemed over. Adrienne was the first to see the road, a muddy swath cut through the brush.

"We made it," she said, turning to Matt in triumph.

"It's just an unpaved farm road, Adrienne. There's a little town maybe thirty or forty miles that way, and I have no idea what's in the other direction."

Adrienne sagged. Thirty or forty miles. She'd never be able to walk it. The road didn't look well-traveled, either. Maybe Matt had been right that no one would come along. All that effort to find this road, and they didn't seem much better off than when they'd been sitting by the edge of the cliff.

"So do we walk or wait?" Matt asked, turning his collar up against the wind that seemed much colder, now that they were standing still.

Adrienne shivered as the chill penetrated her wet clothes. While she'd been moving, she hadn't noticed the cold as much, maybe because then she'd felt as if someone were jabbing hot knives into her feet and calves. "I don't know what to do," she admitted, exhaustion lowering her defenses.

He studied her for a moment. "You're weaving."

She made an effort to stand erect, but it was no use. She hobbled to a low rock near the road and eased herself down to it with a groan. Then she covered her face with both hands to hide her tears.

"Here."

She kept her face covered. "What?"

"It's still damp, but better than nothing."

She felt something being draped around her shoulders. His sport coat. She glanced up and wiped her eyes. "No. You need it."

"I'm okay."

She gazed at him, finally ready to admit that she'd been foolish to insist on this hike through the wilderness. "Matt, I—" She stopped as two pinpricks of light appeared on the road. "A car!" she screeched, leaping up, forgetting her exhaustion. "Here comes a car!"

He turned. "By God, you're right. Let's hope they stop."

"Of course they'll stop. It's probably some nice couple, driving home after dinner and a movie in town. I'm sure that—"

"They're driving home after a night in town, all right, and it must have been some night. Look at them. They're all over the road."

"Drunk?" Adrienne whispered.

"Drunk or asleep at the wheel. Neither one's too good for our situation."

"Dammit, they can't do that to us!"

Matt glanced at her and grinned. "Well, at least your spunk is back. I was worried about you for a while. Looked like you were giving up."

"Well, I'm not." Adrienne walked into the center of the road and began waving her arms.

"Hey!" Matt dragged her back. "They might run you down. You're all in black and they might not even see you."

"But we have to get them to stop," she protested.

"You stand there. I'll flag them down."

"Same old Matt, issuing orders."

"My shirt's white." He grabbed his jacket from her shoulders. "And I can wave this." He walked to the middle of the road and turned back to her. "Unless you care to take off your jacket and wave it?" he asked with a sly look. "That should work."

She rolled her eyes. "Same old Matt."

The lights bobbed closer and Matt waved the coat. "Sounds like a pickup," he said. "He's going slow, so maybe we can jump on the truck bed, even if he doesn't stop."

"I don't know, Matt. I've never—"

"Quiet," Matt ordered, holding up one hand. "What's that noise?"

Adrienne listened and burst out laughing. "Singing."

"Not in my book. This fellow is tanked, let me tell you." Matt waved the jacket and yelled as the lights swerved to one side of the road and then the other.

"Matt, be careful."

He glanced toward the side of the road where she stood. "Worried about me?"

"Never."

"Didn't think so." Matt waved the coat some more and shouted for the truck to stop.

"Matt, watch out!" Adrienne screamed as the truck headed straight toward him.

Matt jumped out of the way just in time, and the truck slammed to a halt.

"You tryin' t'git kilt?" said someone in a cracked, whiskey-laden voice.

Matt walked slowly up to the cab of the battered truck. "We need a ride."

"We?" cackled the voice.

Adrienne crossed the road to stand beside Matt. She estimated the driver of the truck was in his mid-sixties. He wore an old straw hat, sported a chin full of gray, day-old bristles, and nursed a plug of tobacco in one weathered cheek. He smelled like a brewery.

"Me and my companion," Matt said, nodding toward Adrienne.

The old man peered at them, as if trying to focus.

"Jist two of ya? I see a couple more'n two."

"I'll bet he does," Adrienne said under her breath. "Maybe you could drive, Matt."

"We had an accident," Matt explained. "We need a ride to a telephone. You look kind of tired, Mr.—"

"Jist call me Archie."

"Okay, Archie," Matt said. "Anyway, maybe I could drive us back into town, so we can make a phone call. You could rest."

Adrienne crossed her fingers.

"Telephone? Shoot, I got a telephone. Lot closer than town. You two come home with me. Where's yer car?"

"Airplane," Matt said.

"You had a accident in a airplane?" the old man croaked. "You ain't ghosts, are ya?"

"Not ghosts," Matt said, smiling. "Listen, why don't you scoot over, and I'll drive us the rest of the way to your house."

"'Cause I like ghosts okay, but I like t'know when I'm dealin' with 'em," Archie said. "My wife's a ghost, now."

Adrienne tugged on Matt's sleeve. "I don't know about this," she whispered.

"We don't have much choice," he replied in an undertone. Then he spoke to the old man again. "So, would you like a top-notch chauffeur for the next few miles?"

"Nobody drives Bessie but me. Ever'body knows that," Archie said. "Git in, both of ya."

"But I'd be glad to—"

"Either git in, or don't. I'm leavin'." Archie revved the engine.

"We'll get in," Matt said quickly, motioning Adrienne around the back of the truck. As they reached the cab he whispered instructions. "I'll sit next to him, in case I have to grab the wheel."

"Good. Then you can inhale all those fumes, too. The guy reeks."

"Can't look a gift horse in the mouth."

At that moment Adrienne heard the squirt of tobacco juice and the splat of it hitting the road. "Especially in this case," she muttered, grimacing.

They piled into the dilapidated interior of the truck. Bare springs poked Adrienne's backside whenever the truck bounced, and a loose flap of headliner kept tickling her ear. Matt concentrated on Archie and flexed his hands in preparation for wrenching the wheel away from him if necessary.

"You two sing?" Archie asked.

"No," Adrienne and Matt answered together.

"Party poopers," Archie declared. "Might of knowed I'd pick me up a couple party poopers. Then I'll sing, anyway."

Adrienne gripped the door as Archie began a braying chorus of "Roll Me Over in the Clover" and steered the truck toward the edge of the road. In the nick of time, as Matt was about to grab the wheel, Archie corrected his course and moved at a diagonal toward the other side of the road.

As they snaked down the road, with Archie bellowing at the top of his lungs and the upholstery springs jabbing into her bottom, Adrienne kept her sanity by focusing on the telephone that waited at the end of the ride. She squinted at her watch. Almost two in the morning. Her parents would have begun to worry by now, but might not have called the authorities.

After an interminable time, Archie swerved the truck into an opening between two posts. A fainter road led to a ramshackle house and an outbuilding, perhaps a barn. No lights showed, either inside or out.

"Electricity musta blowed out," Archie explained. "Got candles, though. Hafta reset the dang clock."

"We just need the phone," Adrienne said, climbing stiffly down from the cab. "Where is it?"

"Where it's always been, missy." Archie staggered toward the door and pushed it open. "Never lock it," he said, and fumbled with the wall switch. "Electricity's blowed out," he said again and teetered into the room, banging into furniture as he went.

Adrienne peered through the gloom and tried to adjust her eyes to locate the telephone. The room smelled like the musty stacks of a college library. She made out the vague outlines of bookshelves lining an entire wall.

Matt came up behind her. "Do you see it?"

"No, and he won't tell me—wait, there it is," she said, stepping gingerly around the furniture. "On that wall." The telephone hung on a clear space near the door into the kitchen, where Archie was rummaging noisily through drawers. "I can't believe that we're finally out of this crazy situation," Adrienne said. "After we call my parents, maybe we can locate someone to pick us up."

"Maybe. If we can figure out where we are."

"Right." Adrienne lifted the receiver of the black rotary dial phone. "Thank God for the modern age." She listened, and jiggled the button in the cradle. She kept jiggling, but no dial tone sounded. She turned to Matt, the last of her reserves drained. "This can't be happening. The phone's dead."

4

MATT REACHED for the receiver. "Let me try."

"I know a dead phone when I hear one!" Adrienne jerked the receiver away from him and slammed it into the cradle.

"If it wasn't dead before, you just killed it," Matt said. "And don't shout at me. I'm not the one who promised you a telephone at the end of the ride. Ask our friend Archie."

"Let there be light!" Archie crowed, staggering into the living room with a burning candle stuck in a vinegar bottle. In his other hand he held an empty tin can. He lifted the candle toward Adrienne and Matt and peered at them with bloodshot eyes. "You folks don't appear t'be having much fun."

Adrienne groaned. "Why didn't you tell us the phone doesn't work?"

"It don't?" Archie cocked his head to one side. "Well, that's right, it don't. Never works when it rains. Wall gets wet, y'know. Leak somewheres. Never did find where." He spat tobacco juice into the tin can, revealing its purpose. "Wall gets wet—phone don't work." He thought for a moment and then smiled, revealing tobacco-stained teeth. "Works when the wall dries. Should be dry by mornin'."

Adrienne turned away, afraid Matt and Archie would see the tears in her eyes. "That'll be a little too late," she said, and started to shiver. She was cold and wet and Granny would die tonight without her being there, not to mention how worried her parents would be when they didn't hear from her soon.

"Archie, we need a phone," Matt said. "Adrienne has to call her parents. If you'd let us borrow the truck and take it into town—"

"Outta gas," Archie said, and hiccuped.

Adrienne turned back as hope resurfaced. "Maybe not completely out of gas," she said, glancing at Matt. "All we need is enough to get to town. We'll pay you for the use of your truck—" She paused as Matt gave her a warning look. They had no money. "Eventually," she finished, "when we recover our wallets from the plane."

"Outta gas," Archie said, wagging his head back and forth and grinning. "Sittin' on the big E."

"Where are the keys?" Matt persisted. "I can double-check that."

Archie put down the tin can and slapped the pockets of his worn jeans, shifting the vinegar bottle to do so and dripping wax on his hand. "Dang." He put the bottle down and scraped off the wax before slapping his pockets again. "Musta left 'em in Bessie. You go look."

"I'll be right back," Matt said, sending a reassuring glance toward Adrienne.

"Take yer time," Archie said. As Matt dashed out the door, he winked at Adrienne. "Wanna drink?"

"No, thanks." She rubbed her arms and shivered.

"Then I'll git me one." Archie took his tin can and the vinegar bottle and teetered over to a cupboard under a window. "Dorothy called this the likker cab'nit," he said, putting the candle on top and opening a door. "She was refined. I jist call it my booze bin." He brought out a half gallon of whiskey, unscrewed the top, and took a hefty swig from the bottle.

"Do you drink like this all the time?" Adrienne asked, her teeth chattering with cold.

"Mostly," he said, wiping his mouth on his sleeve.

"Why?"

The question seemed to baffle him. "'Cause I like it," he said finally.

She wondered if the alcohol made him immune to the cold. He took another swallow, and she glanced at the door, willing Matt to come through it with good news about the gas gauge. But when he walked into the cabin and looked at her, she knew Archie had been right. The truck was out of gas. She sagged against the kitchen doorjamb.

Matt surveyed the room, which was dimly illuminated by the single candle guarding Archie's liquor supply. "Any chance you have central heating, Archie?"

The old man chuckled. "No chance." He waved his hand toward one wall. "Fireplace."

"Woodpile?" Matt asked.

"Outside," Archie said, and spat into the tin can. "Most likely wet."

"Most likely," Matt said, gazing out the window.

Adrienne walked over to him. "I'm really freezing."

"I can tell. I'll hunt through the woodpile. Maybe at the bottom of the stack there's—"

"In the barn," Archie said as he wobbled toward them. "Scrap wood. Burns real good."

"Great," Matt said, rubbing his hands together. "Got a flashlight?"

Archie jerked his thumb back toward the liquor cabinet. "Got a candle."

Matt glanced at the candle. "All right," he said, and crossed the room to pick it up.

"I'm going with you," Adrienne said. "You can't hold a candle and wood, and besides, the wind and the rain might snuff out the flame. I'll shield it on the way back."

Matt looked at her. "It's *very* muddy out there."

Adrienne stared at him and then down at her ruined clothes and crusted shoes. She began to laugh. "No kidding," she said and started for the door.

Once outside, she regretted her bravado. The cabin had been cold; the air outside was freezing. Besides, Matt hadn't exaggerated about the mud. The well-trod area between the house and the barn had soaked up the rain more than the untracked wilds they'd trudged through after the crash landing. Her heels sank two inches into the muck and came out again with a sucking sound. "This is worse than I thought," she said, breathing hard.

"Hold my hand."

She did, and was grateful for its steadying pressure. The candle flame flickered but didn't go out as they slopped through the mud toward the structure Archie had called a barn. Adrienne thought it looked more like a large, tin-roofed shed. Her parents had a real barn, painted dark red, with a hayloft. Her parents were in that barn now, with Granny. She'd probably never see Granny alive again.

"You okay?" Matt asked.

"Why?"

He held up their clasped hands. "You've got me in a death grip."

"Oh. Sorry." She relaxed her fingers and tried to wiggle them from his grasp.

"Hey, don't go schizy on me. I didn't say you couldn't hang on," he said, locking his fingers through hers.

She stopped struggling and savored the secure contact until they reached the barn, where he handed her the candle and used both hands to push up the wooden bar holding the double doors closed. Then he swung the doors out, and they were greeted by the toasty smell of fresh straw. Adrienne swallowed a lump in her throat. This barn smelled like the one at home, even if it didn't look much like it.

She held the candle as they stepped inside. The shed was surprisingly clean and weather-tight, with no evident leaks after the heavy rain. The concrete floor had recently been swept. The shed contained two stalls on their left, and shelves full of odds and ends on their right. Both stalls were empty, but one had been recently laid with the straw that Adrienne had smelled when they'd opened the doors. Several of the weathered boards forming the sides of the stall had been replaced with new pine, which added to the pleasant fragrance.

"Looks like Archie's expecting a four-footed visitor," Adrienne said, motioning to the refurbished stall.

"And from the look of the picks and shovels over here, I'll make a guess that it's a burro or mule, something for prospecting," Matt added. "Somehow I'm not surprised."

"He's a real backwoods character, all right." Adrienne held the candle aloft. "Look, a kerosene lantern."

"If our luck holds, it won't have any kerosene," Matt said, reaching for the rusty handle. He shook the lantern and a sloshing sound came from the base. "Then again, maybe our luck's about to change." He replaced the lantern on the shelf and lifted the glass chimney. "It's even got a wick," he muttered.

Adrienne handed him the candle, and in another moment he'd lit the lantern and adjusted the wick so the interior of the barn glowed with soft light. "That's so much better," Adrienne said with a sigh. "It doesn't seem as cold, somehow."

"It's not as cold. Old Archie's place is tight as a drum, and there aren't any windows to let out the heat." Matt held the lantern up to Adrienne's face. "You know, Burnham, you're a mess."

"How nice of you to notice. You don't look so spiffy, yourself."

"Probably not," he said with a chuckle, "but I don't wear mascara so I don't have raccoon eyes."

She bristled. "Oh, you think my smeared makeup looks funny, do you?"

"Yep."

"This comment comes from a guy who exposed his red underwear to an entire roomful of people?"

Matt laughed. "You're sharp, Burnham. You also take life far too seriously." He picked up the lantern. "Come on, let's locate the scrap wood Archie told us about."

By the time they returned to the house, Matt with an armload of splintered planks and Adrienne with the lantern, Archie had a second candle going, this time stuck in a catsup bottle. He sprawled in a worn leather easy chair and cradled his whiskey. "See ya found the boards. Tore 'em out to fix up the stall for my new burro. Seth's bringing her. Gonna name her Dorothy the third. See, m'wife was Dorothy the first, my old burro was Dorothy the second, so this'll be Dorothy the third."

"I see." Adrienne wondered how his wife would have felt about having burros named after her. "We found your lantern," she added, moving some old newspapers aside and setting the lantern on a heavy wooden coffee table.

"That's my prospectin' lantern," Archie said gruffly. "Don't be usin' too much of the kerosene, now. Might need it when I git my burro. Dorothy the third."

"If we use too much we'll buy you some more," Adrienne said, protective of her new source of light. "Eventually," she added, remembering that she still had no money, credit cards or transportation out of this remote hideaway.

Matt unloaded his armload of wood by the large rock fireplace and walked over to the coffee table. "Mind if I use those newspapers to start the fire, Archie?"

"'Course I mind."

Matt stopped in the act of reaching for the papers. "You do?"

"Them's Dorothy's. Dorothy the first."

Matt glanced at him. "But isn't Dorothy. . .?"

"A ghost?" Archie finished. "Shore is. But them's her newspapers, with her crosswords in 'em, and nobody's burnin' nothin' of Dorothy's."

"Okay," Matt said, "then what can I use?"

"Don't fret about lightin' the fire. You pile the boards in there. I'll light it."

"With what?"

"I'll light it," Archie repeated.

Matt shrugged and turned back to the fireplace. Soon he had the wood in the fireplace and the flue open.

"Jist stand back," Archie said, and heaved himself, whiskey bottle and all, out of the chair. He staggered to an end table, opened a narrow drawer, and took out a metal tin.

Matt gazed at him as the old man shook some white powder into his hand and walked toward the fireplace. "Hey, Archie, can I have a drink of your whiskey?" he asked.

Adrienne groaned. Now Matt would start on the booze and she'd have two inebriated men on her hands. "Matt, if you'd wait until—"

"Shore can," Archie said, swinging the bottle in Matt's direction.

Matt grabbed the bottle and then Adrienne's arm, propelling her to the other side of the room, away from the fireplace.

"What in the name of heaven do you think you're doing?" she asked, struggling unsuccessfully in his iron grip. "If you think that you can start boozing it up and then get cute with me, you have another think coming."

"Stay here," Matt commanded, holding her tight. "He's going to light that thing with gunpowder."

Openmouthed, Adrienne stared at him. "Gunpowder?" she croaked.

"Uh-huh." He hoisted the bottle in her direction. "Care for a drink?"

Just then Archie tossed a match into the fireplace and a whoosh of flame sent him staggering back. "Damnation," he said, "must've put too much."

Adrienne gazed wide-eyed at the crackling fire. She turned her face up to Matt's. "Gunpowder?" she mouthed again.

"It's an old frontier trick I saw demonstrated once, not particularly dangerous unless you don't know what you're doing, or you're holding a jug of booze and you're three sheets to the wind."

Adrienne took a deep breath. "And here I thought you had decided to join Archie in his drinking spree. You've come to my rescue again, Matt." She glanced up at him. "I guess that makes up for the crack about raccoon eyes."

"Which you still have," he said with a smile, giving her arm a friendly squeeze.

"Not for long." Disengaging herself from Matt, she approached Archie with caution, unsure if all the gunpowder had been burned. The heat from the fireplace felt wonderful, though, and she began to relax. "I was wondering," she began, looking sideways at the grizzled old man, "if I could wash up in your bathroom."

Archie turned his head and studied her from her toes to the top of her head. "Appears you need more than that," he said, shifting his tobacco to the opposite cheek. "You look like somethin' the cat drug in."

Adrienne grimaced. She was getting compliments right and left. It was enough to turn a girl's head. "All my stuff's in the airplane," she said. "Washing up is all I can do right now."

Archie continued to stare at her, and finally he began to nod.

"So it's okay? Where—" Adrienne began.

"Hold on, missy. Might as well do this proper. But you gotta promise t'be careful."

"Well, of course I—"

"Don't tear nothin'."

"Tear?"

"Dorothy's clothes. I'm gonna let you wear some of 'em, long as you promise to be careful."

"Oh, I couldn't borrow your wife's things," Adrienne protested, even as the thought of dry, clean clothes cradled her like a reassuring hug.

"Yep, you could," Archie said, and wheeled around abruptly to face Matt. "How'd you like that whiskey?"

"Great," Matt said.

"Have you another swig."

"Thanks." Matt tipped the bottle to his lips and swallowed.

"You don't look much better'n her," Archie said, giving Matt the once-over, too. "When I git her fixed up," he said, jerking his head toward Adrienne, "I'll find somethin' fer you. I don't figure you'd be as careful as her, but it'll be my clothes, so it don't matter much."

Matt shook his head. "That's okay," he said. "I'll be fine. You don't have to—"

"Hush up," Archie said, fastening his hand around Adrienne's wrist, "and take care of my whiskey while I go look for somethin' for yer sweetheart." He picked up the lantern on his way by the coffee table, and pulling Adrienne along, headed for a doorway a little past Matt.

"I'm not his sweetheart," Adrienne said. She noticed that Matt was grinning at her. "Tell him I'm not your sweetheart."

Matt didn't say a word, just kept smiling at her. She watched him over her shoulder, perplexed by the look in his eyes, until the lantern light no longer shone on his face. If someone had asked her to describe the emotion she'd seen in his expression, she would have said it was tenderness, the kind that usually takes time to develop. They'd known each other a few hours, no more. Yet she had to admit that they'd packed a lot into those few hours.

"Kept Dorothy's clothes just like she left 'em," Archie said, leading Adrienne past a four-poster bed to a mahogany armoire. He released her wrist and flung open the doors. "There," he said, turning to her expectantly. "Most anythin' you need."

The scent of violets floated into the room. Adrienne gazed upon the "most anythin'" and saw three faded housedresses in flowered prints, a quilted blue bathrobe, a high-necked flannel nightgown, two pairs of worn jeans, a blue chambray skirt and three western-style blouses. A modest wardrobe, and yet Archie presented it as if he were offering her the latest collection from Dior.

"She liked this'n best," Archie said, unhooking the blue chambray skirt. "See? Lace."

Adrienne looked closer in the light from the lantern and noticed that the skirt's hem was trimmed with a narrow border of lace. "Very pretty," she said.

"Here." Archie thrust the skirt into her arms. "Now where's that top she had? In the drawer, most likely." He leaned down and opened one of two drawers at the base of the armoire. "Nope. Just mentionables."

Adrienne smiled. He probably meant "unmentionables"—his wife's underwear.

Archie opened the bottom drawer. "Yep. Here's the top goes with that skirt." He pulled out a white eyelet blouse and unfolded it. He held it up. "Yep." He gazed at the blouse for a long time.

"You cared for her a lot, didn't you?" Adrienne ventured.

"That ornery woman?" Archie snorted. "Always tryin' to educate me about some fool thing or other. She was a tolerable lot of trouble, that's what."

Adrienne kept silent. She didn't believe a word of his tirade, but she thought he'd be embarrassed to admit to her how much he loved and missed his wife.

"Take this," Archie said, handing her the blouse. "Goes with the skirt."

"I'm not sure this is the right thing to do. I can see no one's disturbed her things since . . . since . . ."

Archie gazed at her with bloodshot eyes. "She'd a wanted me to let you wear her clothes. She was hard

enough to live with in life. Don't want her ghost harpin'
on me, too."

"Well, I—thanks."

"How 'bout them mentionables?"

Adrienne hesitated. Every stitch she had on was
soaked through, but she didn't want to presume too
much.

"Take some," Archie said, opening the top drawer
again. "And git out of them torture stilts you got on yer
feet," he added, reaching in the back of the armoire and
producing a pair of soft moccasins. "Bathroom's in
yonder. Shower, sink . . . everythin'." He waved toward a door off the bedroom. "I'm leavin' the light."
Then he stomped out of the bedroom muttering that he
was long overdue for a drink. He closed the door behind him.

Adrienne peered into the drawer of "mentionables"
and found that in this department Dorothy had
splurged. She'd chosen her outer clothes to conform to
life in the wilderness, but underneath she clung to luxury in the form of silk camisoles and tap pants in several pastel shades. In one corner of the drawer Adrienne
saw a lingerie catalog. So that was how Dorothy had
shopped. Adrienne wondered how old she'd been when
she died. Archie looked old, but constant sun and
plenty of whiskey could age someone fast.

Choosing an ivory set of tap pants and camisole,
Adrienne ventured into the bathroom. She was surprised to find it was clean. Archie didn't strike her as
the kind of man who would scrub bathrooms. After
taking out her rhinestone earrings, she stripped off her

clothes and threw them in a pile. After tonight's escapade they'd be fit only for rags.

The hot shower on her chilled skin made her moan with pleasure. A two-tiered, plastic shelf hung from the shower head, and on it was a bar of yellow soap and a bottle of Johnson's Baby Shampoo. Archie and Johnson's Baby Shampoo made an interesting combination, she thought as she quickly used some to wash her hair.

After that she wasted no time soaping and rinsing her body, guessing that a house out in the middle of nowhere wouldn't have an unlimited supply of hot water. After all that Matt had done for her, including the gunpowder incident, he deserved a shower, too. She turned off the water and dried herself on a clean but raggedy pink towel. Then, and only then, she allowed herself to look in the medicine cabinet mirror.

The raccoon eyes were gone, but so was the rest of her makeup. As a blonde with fair lashes and pale skin, she'd always thought she needed a lot of it, especially to foster her image as a sophisticated businesswoman. That image had just been washed down the drain, unless Dorothy had left cosmetics behind, too.

On the off chance that she had, Adrienne opened the medicine chest and the cabinet under the sink. She found deodorant and a bottle of body lotion but no makeup. She hadn't really expected to find any after looking over Dorothy's utilitarian wardrobe.

She returned to the bedroom and dressed quickly. The chambray skirt was a little loose, but otherwise the clothes fit reasonably well. As she sat on the bed to put on the soft moccasins, she noticed a dressing table in one corner. A silver-plated comb and brush, obviously Dorothy's, lay on one side of the table along with a partly filled atomizer.

On the other side of the table perched a five-by-seven silver picture frame. Adrienne crossed to the table and sat on the needlepoint-cushioned stool. She picked up the picture and studied it. Archie was in the middle of the picture, holding the halter of a shaggy burro which stood on his left. Archie's other arm was wrapped securely around the shoulders of a woman who looked to be twenty years younger than he was. She had light brown hair cut short and a sweet face, which she'd turned toward Archie as she gave him a wistful smile. She wore the same chambray skirt and white eyelet blouse that Adrienne had on. So this was Dorothy. She certainly didn't look ornery.

Adrienne had a hard time imagining these two together, and yet obviously they'd shared a special kind of love. She positioned the frame carefully, cocking it at the same angle as she'd found it. After some hesitation she used the comb and brush on her tangled hair. Then she retrieved her towel and wiped the set before replacing it on the table. She held the atomizer to her nose and sniffed. The cologne had the same scent of violets that had wafted from the armoire. Dorothy, she decided, had been a secret romantic.

Adrienne put down the atomizer without using any of the cologne. If left there it would eventually evaporate, but until it did, Archie would retain the sweet scent he remembered. Adrienne had a hunch he needed that.

Picking up her tattered clothes and folding them into a bundle, she opened the bedroom door. Archie's raspy voice drifted from the living room, as he delivered a tale about prospecting for gold, and Matt sounded as if he was egging him on. Adrienne approached silently, her moccasins making no sound on the hardwood floor. She found the two men sitting like old friends, each in an easy chair in front of the fire. Archie passed his whiskey bottle to Matt, who took a swig.

Adrienne regretted rushing her shower. Matt looked perfectly comfortable boozing it up with Archie, as if he hadn't a care in the world, as if his plane weren't lying at the bottom of some canyon, and his passenger desperately trying to contact her parents. In another hour he and Archie probably would be asleep in those same chairs, leaving her alone to worry and wait.

"The shower's free," she said louder than she'd meant to.

Matt turned to gaze at her. She'd expected some smart crack about the raccoon eyes being gone, or that she looked about twelve years old without makeup. Instead he said nothing, and his lips curved in a soft smile. She concluded that he must be drunk.

Archie took a can of tobacco from his shirt pocket and replenished the wad in his cheek. "Right nice," he said, nodding. "Not as nice as Dorothy looked, but right nice."

"I appreciate the clothes," Adrienne said, becoming uncomfortable under Matt's quiet assessment. She held up the bundle containing her black suit, shoes and underwear. "These are done for." She glanced at Matt. "I'd think you'd want to change, too."

"What?" He seemed to come out of a daze. "Oh, yeah. I would." He stood up quickly, too quickly for someone who was inebriated.

Adrienne revised her opinion. No telling what was the matter with him, but he was acting as if he'd lost every brain cell in his head.

"I'll git you some duds," Archie said, hauling himself out of the chair. "Got some things I've outgrowed," he added, patting his stomach.

Matt gestured toward the chair. "Sit here," he said to Adrienne, "and get warm."

"Thank you." She watched his expression as she passed him to take the chair he'd vacated. Sure enough, the soft little smile appeared again. He'd definitely lost his mind.

Archie and Matt trekked off to the bedroom together while Adrienne sank against the worn leather of the chair and wondered why she felt so terrific. For the moment, anyway, in this cozy cabin with Matt and Archie, she felt contentment steal over her.

She admonished herself for relaxing. She should be brainstorming ways to get out of here. But the warmth of the fire reached around her, coaxing her to nestle down in the chair, to lean her head back, to close her eyes. . . .

A SOUND LIKE A bear's growl woke her, and she cried out, disoriented.

"It's okay," Matt soothed, stepping forward from where he'd been leaning against the fireplace, apparently watching her. "Archie's snoring, that's all. Go back to sleep."

Adrienne glanced to the other chair. Archie lolled in it, his head back, his mouth open. The sound came again, like someone dragging a load of railroad ties across a rutted road. "Good Lord."

Matt chuckled. "My dad snores like that. Shakes the whole house. Mom says sleeping with him is worse than living beside an airport. She wears earplugs to bed."

"I don't think earplugs would make a dent in that racket," Adrienne said, returning her attention to Matt. For the first time she took a good look at him. The clothes Archie had "outgrowed" fit Matt like a second skin. He had on a black western shirt fastened with pearlized snaps. The yoke of the shirt emphasized the breadth of his shoulders, and the tight jeans brought her attention to his lean hips.

"What's the smile for?" Matt asked. "Haven't you ever seen a cowboy before?"

"Um, sure. I just didn't picture you as one," Adrienne replied, wondering if the smile she quickly suppressed in any way resembled the one she'd seen on Matt earlier.

"I didn't picture you as a country girl, either," Matt said, "but there you are."

Adrienne held his gaze. No doubt about it, she was once again experiencing the emotion she'd felt when he'd kissed her beside the wash. Except that now she was out of immediate danger, and warm, and relaxed. He took a step toward her, but stopped when another blast emerged from the opposite chair.

"And there *he* is," she said, brought back to the reality of their situation. "What time is it, anyway?"

"A little after three," Matt said, consulting his watch.

Adrienne groaned. "My parents have probably alerted the authorities by now. I hate not being able to contact them. Can't you think of a way?"

"Unfortunately, no. While you were sleeping and Archie was finishing off his bottle, I tried to come up with some solution. Without a telephone or gas for the truck, we're kind of stuck."

Another loud snore from Archie brought Adrienne's attention back to the sleeping old man. "Why would he drive home on an empty tank?"

"I asked him that when you were in the shower. He has this problem all the time, because he drives into town, gets smashed, and isn't ready to leave until the only station in Saddlehorn is closed for the night. One of the reasons he's buying this burro is to get him out of jams like this."

"Saddlehorn? That's the name of the nearest town?"

"Apparently."

"I've never heard of it," Adrienne said, speaking loud enough to be heard over Archie's snoring.

"I vaguely remember seeing it on an aerial map, but it's not much of a place, I don't think."

"Still, they'd have a telephone, if we could get there."

"That's a big *if*." He gazed at her. "I'm sorry about this, Adrienne. Really sorry. I should have let you take a commercial flight. You'd be there by now."

She shook her head. "I won't let you blame yourself, not with your plane at the bottom of the canyon. We both lost out, that's all. I just feel so helpless."

"Me, too. I've gone around and around on this, but I can't think of a way out. Maybe we'd better follow Archie's example and try to get some sleep."

Archie's snoring grew louder yet.

"I think I'd need a jug of whiskey in me before I could sleep through that," Adrienne said.

"Maybe if you went into his bedroom and closed the door?"

"You're welcome to try," Adrienne said. "I'll take the barn. That stall with a fresh bed of straw and a blanket should work fine."

Matt grinned. "I thought *I'd* take the barn."

"But you're the one used to snoring. You said so."

"I never said that. My mother's used to it. When I was eleven I soundproofed my room with acoustical tile."

"We could flip a coin," Adrienne suggested.

"Or," Matt said, leaning casually against the mantel as the firelight played across the lean contours of his body, "we could both sleep in the barn."

5

"I DON'T THINK that's a good idea, Matt." Adrienne shifted in her chair and glanced away.

"I didn't think you would."

"I mean, considering that I met you only a few hours ago, I hardly think it's a proper thing to be sharing a blanket in a barn."

"Highly improper," Matt said, his hazel eyes challenging her. "So I guess you'll be staying in here?"

She looked at him. "*You* could stay in here and let me have the barn."

"Afraid not. You see, I don't object to sharing a blanket with you, you object to sharing a blanket with me."

"It's not that I object, as if you were an objectionable person. I don't think it's wise—we hardly know each other," Adrienne protested. "You make me sound like such a prude."

"Oh, you do a fine job of sounding that way without my help."

"I am not a prude!"

Archie snuffled and snorted before launching into another loud snore.

"I'm going to look for a blanket," Matt said.

Adrienne sat rigidly in the chair. She didn't want to stay in the house and listen to Archie snore for the rest of the night. Truthfully, she didn't want to leave Matt's side, either. She felt safer when he was around, except in one respect, and that was the respect that had her worried about going to the barn with him.

Not that she thought he'd force his attentions on her. No, *force* wasn't Matt's style, but *persuade* most definitely was, and she doubted her strength to resist after all they'd been through, and considering how sexy he looked in the snug western shirt and jeans.

But Adrienne wasn't the kind of woman who succumbed to a man she'd known for only a matter of hours. Such behavior didn't fit her self-image, but it didn't make her a prude, as she'd tried to explain to Matt while he'd continued to give her that irritating, and very sexy, smile of his.

Matt appeared carrying two blankets. One was a gray, white and black geometric pattern and the other was woven in shades of brown. "See you in the morning." He picked up the lantern and started toward the door.

"Matt . . ."

He turned, and Archie blasted forth with the loudest snore Adrienne had heard yet.

She stood up and faced him. The light from the kerosene lantern highlighted his cheekbones and the fullness of his lower lip, but cast his eyes into shadow. He looked mysterious and far too inviting. "You understand that if I go out there with you, it means nothing. I'm only getting away from the noise."

He shrugged. "Sure," he agreed, but the faint smile reappeared.

Adrienne hesitated a moment longer. "Okay. As long as we understand each other."

"We understand each other."

"Good."

"You'd better put the grate over the fire before we leave," Matt said.

She did. She had to admit that he kept his head about things like that, whereas she seemed to have lost hers. She'd forgotten that the fire, although it was little more than embers now, still needed to be contained. It was his coolness under pressure that made her trust him...in all matters but one.

She walked toward the door. "Let's go."

"Wrap this around you," he instructed, holding out the brown blanket. "No sense in getting chilled."

The wool blanket repelled the cold as he opened the door. She hugged it tightly around her shoulders as they stepped out on the porch. The rain had stopped and a few stars winked through the scudding clouds.

"Storm's over," Matt said, and descended the wooden steps. "Whoops. Forgot about the mud. Hold this," he commanded, handing her the lantern.

"Why?"

"You can't walk through that in Dorothy's moccasins."

"But—" Before she could say more, he'd swept her up in his arms. "These strong-arm tactics are becoming an irritating habit," she muttered, forced by the circumstances to put one arm around his neck to steady herself as he marched across the yard.

"This isn't for your sake," Matt assured her, his breath making clouds in the night air. "Archie trusted you with Dorothy's stuff, and we're not going to repay him by soaking the moccasins and the hem of her skirt in the mud."

She admitted to herself that he had a point, but being carried in his arms, where she could feel his heartbeat against her breast, wasn't helping her keep the necessary distance between them. His hair smelled of Johnson's Baby Shampoo and his cheek of shaving lotion. She decided not to think about why he might have borrowed Archie's razor, because thoughts like those started a quickening within her that promised to further sabotage her resolve.

"I think it's dry enough here by the door, under the overhang," Matt said as he gently lowered her feet to the ground. He opened the door. "M'lady," he said, gesturing toward the interior of the barn.

As she walked into the barn she couldn't shake the feeling that this was like having an illicit rendezvous. When he closed the door, a shiver of anticipation skittered up her spine.

"We'll use the gray and white blanket on the bottom," Matt said, shaking it out over the straw. "It's heavier, almost like a rug. Your blanket can be our cover."

"What about the lantern? Shall I blow it out?"

"If you do, it'll be dark as pitch in here, with no windows." He squatted down to adjust the blanket before settling back on his heels to survey the barn. "Let's put it in the middle of the concrete floor and leave it on low. Waking up in a strange and completely dark room can be scary."

"I didn't think anything scared you."

He stood and walked toward her. "You really think I'm some sort of daredevil, don't you?"

"Aren't you?" she asked, gazing up at him.

"Not nearly as much as you think. But I do believe in taking chances once in a while. Life isn't worth living if you go by the rule book all the time."

"Breaking the rules can make a mess of people's lives," she countered, trying not to be softened by the gentle light and the scent of fresh straw that reminded her so much of home. Sentimental sadness threatened to overwhelm her, and here was this man, so near, with strong arms to comfort her, lips to kiss away her cares, and a willingness to do so, from the look in his eyes.

"Why do you suppose Bev thought we'd get along?" he asked, studying her.

"Beverly?" With all that had happened to them, Adrienne had almost forgotten Beverly, the *friend* who'd helped get her into this mess by inviting Matt to the party and then vouching for his piloting ability. "I have no idea. She knows how conservative I am, and apparently what a risk-taker you are. She couldn't have brought two more unlikely people together."

"Are you sorry?"

She thought about that. If she could turn back the clock and decide to take a commercial flight to Utah, she might be there right now. But then she'd also have to give up everything that had happened tonight, and miserable though she'd been at the time, the new sensation of meeting and conquering danger had somehow exhilarated her.

"Well, I can see why you might be sorry," Matt said, looking disappointed. "It doesn't look like you'll get home tonight."

"No, it doesn't." She felt guilty about the regret in his eyes. "But I'm not sorry I met you. We've had some terrible moments tonight, but because we made it through, I feel stronger, more alive. I guess that's why people do things like skydiving."

"Now you're talking," Matt said, some of his enthusiasm returning.

"Not that I want to try such a thing," she said quickly.

Matt laughed. "Okay. We'll hold off on that." His laugh faded into a gentle smile. "I like the way that blouse and skirt look on you. Quite a transformation from the sophisticated lady I met at the cocktail party. You seem more real, somehow."

"This is as real as it gets," she said, attempting to turn aside the compliment with an offhand remark. "No makeup, no jewelry, no—"

"No pretense," he finished. "Maybe that's it. We're both down to the basics, away from the usual games men and women play, dressing up for each other, being witty, trying to impress. We've been so focused on surviving that we haven't had time for all that phony stuff."

"That phony stuff acts as a protection, sometimes."

"If that's what you want."

She sighed. "I think I do. I probably need protection from someone like—"

"No, you don't," he said softly, reaching for her.

"Wait a minute." Her heart beat in her ears as he drew her into his arms. "Back in the house, you said we understood each other."

"We do." He slid his fingers into her hair and studied her face.

"Then you understand that I don't want this."

He smiled and angled his head toward hers.

"Matt, I don't want you to kiss me."

He gazed into her eyes. "Remember that taking chances makes you feel alive. This is safer than skydiving."

"I've taken enough chances in the past few hours to last me for years."

"Then tell me no," he murmured, coming closer.

Her heart thundered as she tried to form the word. Her lips parted, but no sound came out.

"Here's to taking risks," he said, and held her head still for his kiss.

She sighed one final protest as he claimed her mouth, but she'd known this would happen from the moment he'd closed the door and created this hideaway, perhaps from the moment she'd awakened and found him standing by the fireplace.

He held her tight, imprinting his shape against her, teaching her how to move in concert with him. Excitement skidded through her as the heat from his body fueled hers and an insistent thrumming began deep inside her. His hand splayed across the small of her back as he molded her body against his. The thrumming pulsed faster.

He lifted his mouth a fraction from hers. "Lie with me," he whispered.

She was helpless to resist as he guided her gently down onto the blanket. His desires had become hers. He held her gaze as he unfastened the buttons of the eyelet blouse slowly and carefully. He parted the material. She took a shuddering breath as his glance moved downward over the ivory camisole. Her breasts thrust against the material; he'd have no doubt that she wanted him. She flushed, knowing her desire was plain to see.

His gaze returned to hers and he touched her cheek. "There's nothing to be ashamed of," he murmured.

"But this . . . this isn't like me."

"How do you know?" He brushed his palm over the tip of her breast as he looked deep into her eyes. "Are you so sure of everything about yourself?"

"Not anymore," she whispered.

He leaned down, his mouth hovering close to hers. "Good," he said, before settling into a kiss that took her breath away.

In a response as uncontrollable as her heartbeat, she arched upward against the pressure of his hand cupping her breast and parted her lips to invite his tongue inside. She could no more halt the revealing movements of her body than she could cease breathing. When he slipped his hand beneath the camisole, she moaned in delight as he caressed her heated skin. Her initial shame disappeared, replaced with a fiery longing that had her tugging at snaps and pulling his shirt free.

He lifted his head and laughed hoarsely in his throat. "Easy," he said, his breath ragged. "Don't want to rip Archie's shirt, either."

Her hands stilled. "What is happening to me?" she murmured, gazing up at him. "I've never been this aggressive with a man."

"It's the danger we've been in," he said, stroking her breast until she closed her eyes in pleasure. "Danger sharpens your senses."

"But I don't like danger."

He eased the camisole up and kissed her bare skin. "Do you like this?"

She moaned as he drew her nipple into his mouth. Passion erupted within her, a passion that made her tremble and gasp his name.

He lifted his head to gaze at her. "That's what I wanted. Lose control, Adrienne."

"I can't help myself," she whispered.

"Why should you? We're all alone. We can please ourselves in any way we want, and there's no one to tell us we can't." He pushed up her skirt and pressed his hand between her thighs, sending shock waves through her.

Her words were choked. "I want you."

"I know," he said gently. The soft buzz of his zipper made her writhe in expectation. The crackle of cellophane told her he'd somehow managed to obtain birth control, a small miracle she didn't stop to question.

Slowly he nuzzled his way back to her lips. "We're going to make beautiful love," he whispered against her mouth.

"Yes." Delirious with need, she accepted his deep kiss and burrowed into the sensuality of his touch. As he drew the tap pants down, she nudged them away. "Love me, Matt," she whispered, opening her thighs, rising to meet his first thrust.

His groan of pleasure filled the small barn and excited her even more. She met his passion with cries of her own as the tension mounted. Panting, he pushed her onward, building toward a shared climax that left them slick with moisture and gasping for breath. Adrienne even imagined she heard the clang of a gong.

Slowly she realized the sound hadn't been an imagined part of their tumultuous lovemaking. Still half-dressed, Matt hadn't taken off his boots. In his energetic movements, he'd kicked something metal with his foot.

"What did you kick?" she murmured.

"I don't know. Never mind." He kissed the hollow of her throat. "Don't think of anything. Just feel."

"Look and see."

"For heaven's—oh, all right." He glanced behind him. "Just a gas can," he said, tracing her lips with his tongue. "Kiss me. I've never known such wonderful lips as yours."

"A gas can," she breathed. "Just a—wait a minute. Did you say a gas can?"

"I know Archie shouldn't have left it here with all this straw, but the lantern is far enough away," Matt said, stroking her hip. "It's probably empty, anyway. Relax, Adrienne. This is so good. Stay with me a moment. Let me savor the—"

"Matt, *a gas can*," she said, pushing at his chest. "There might be gas in it. We have to check."

"In a minute. Adrienne, you're so vibrant, so—"

"Don't you understand?" She shoved him away and rolled out from under him. "If there's gas in that can, we can drive to town!"

Matt plopped face down on the blanket with a groan. "A gas can."

"Yes." Adrienne scrambled over to the side of the stall, where Matt's booted foot had connected with a rusted orange container. She picked it up and liquid sloshed inside. The can was more than half full. "There's gas in it," she announced, grabbing her tap pants where they'd landed amidst the straw. She shook them and put them on. "Let's go." She glanced down to where Matt still lay on the blanket. "I said let's go," she repeated, tucking in her camisole and rebuttoning her blouse.

Matt's voice was muffled by the blanket. "Give me a minute."

"Matt, every minute counts!"

"Don't I know it." He eased himself to his feet with his back to her. After some fumbling and muttering, he sighed and began fastening the snaps of his shirt with a series of popping noises. Then he slowly tucked the shirt inside his jeans and fastened the button at his waist.

"Matt, could you please hurry?"

"For a man in my condition, this *is* hurrying." The zipper's buzz almost drowned out his soft oath. Then he turned. "I had a few things to take care of," he said, gazing at her with desire still in his eyes.

She remembered the crinkle of cellophane. "Oh. Of course." Her cheeks grew hot. "Sorry I was so abrupt. I hope everything . . ."

"Everything is fine. Now if you'll wrap up in the brown blanket and hold the gas can, I'll carry you to the truck."

"All right."

"Then I'll come back, take the lantern into the house, and write a note to Archie, in case he wakes and finds his truck gone. I wouldn't want him to think we stole it."

"Of course not. You're right." Adrienne wrapped the blanket around her. She felt contrite. How could she be so insensitive?

He shook the gray blanket and folded it. Then he walked to the door, opened it and took a steadying breath. "Ready?" he asked, glancing back at her.

"Sure." She came toward him, heart beating, and unceremoniously he picked her up. Even so, the feel of his body against hers started the sizzle all over again. "Matt, I really am sorry," she said again.

"Mmm." He stepped into the cold air.

"Now that I think of it, where did you get that, anyway?"

"Archie."

Her mouth fell open. "Archie?"

"Remember that he assumes we're lovers. He figured we'd lost that item in the plane wreck, too."

"Well, all right. That makes sense, but I still don't understand why Archie would have . . . I mean, is Archie anticipating having girlfriends so soon after his wife died?"

"No. He may never look at another woman, from what he told me while you were asleep. He used condoms when he was married to Dorothy. She was quite a bit younger than Archie, so she was perfectly capable of getting pregnant. They didn't want her to, though, because she had a congenital heart defect. They figured having a baby would be too rough on her."

"That's not what killed her, is it?"

"No. Even with all their precautions, she had a heart attack anyway. Archie told me she was only forty-two."

"How sad."

"The end was sad, but the marriage must have been great. Even though he complains about her, you can tell he was crazy about her."

"Yes, it's really sweet, how much they loved each other." Adrienne realized Matt had stopped walking. They'd reached the truck, but he still cradled her as if he had no intention of depositing her on the passenger seat. She gazed into his eyes. Even in the shadowed light, she could see the glimmer of desire. "I'll open the door, so you can put me down."

"I don't want to put you down. I want—"

She touched her finger to his lips. "I know. But we have to go." Fighting her response to him, she focused on her mother and father, and of course Granny. "We really have to."

"Yeah." He held her gaze a moment longer. "Okay. Open the door."

She reached out and pulled on the cold handle. The door opened with a creak and Matt deposited her on the brittle seat of the pickup.

"Give me the gas can," he said. "I'll look for a funnel while I'm inside." She handed him the can and he slammed the truck's door. Once he was gone, she wrapped the blanket around her and began to shiver.

Until that moment she hadn't really felt the chill. She watched him plow through the mud back to the barn, where he retrieved the lantern and closed the door.

She longed to be back inside the warm barn, back in Matt's arms, feeling his hands all over her. But what was she thinking? She hardly knew this man. This behavior reminded her of . . . of her sisters!

Adrienne shuddered, and not from the cold this time. Whatever impulses had driven her sisters to make terrible mistakes were driving her now, and she had to put a halt to the stampede toward disaster. In her defense, it had taken a plane crash and being stranded in the middle of nowhere to make her forget herself, but forget herself she had.

The driver's door to the old truck opened and Matt climbed inside. "All set," he said, reaching for the key still dangling from the ignition, where Archie had left it.

"You put the gas in already?"

"Didn't you hear me?"

"No, I . . . I was thinking."

"That scares me." He turned the key and the engine caught. "Atta baby," he crooned to the truck, and put it in reverse. "Do I dare ask what you were thinking about?"

"My sisters."

"Excuse me?"

"They're both divorced."

Matt wheeled the truck through the opening in the fence and started down the deserted dirt road. "That's too bad, but I still don't get what you're leading up to."

"They're divorced because they let themselves get carried away with—" She hesitated. No need to insult the man who was driving her to the town she so desperately needed to reach. "With men they should never have married." The truck bounced over a rut and the springs of the seat poked her. Just as well, she thought. She needed a pinch of reality.

Matt glanced at her. "I begin to understand. You feel you've abandoned yourself to a man who would never do as a husband."

"Well, obviously it's not the same—"

"But nobody's said a word about marriage," Matt interrupted, his jaw tight. "Not that you have enough information to judge whether I'd be a suitable candidate."

"That's true, I don't. Which means I don't have enough information to make love to you, either, but I did."

"You won't make love to a guy unless you think you might marry him?"

"Sounds pretty archaic to you, doesn't it?"

He was silent for a minute. "Let's just say that after what happened in the barn, I'm a little surprised."

"That's the very point I'm trying to make. That wasn't like me. I don't know exactly what made me act so out of character. Maybe it was the danger, as you said, and the stress we've been under. But the stress is over, and I can see that nothing good can come out of our continuing what we started back there."

"Because I'm not husband material?"

The truck jounced again and she grimaced. "I wouldn't have stated it that bluntly, but yes."

"Not that I'd ask anybody as tight-assed as you to marry me, but out of curiosity, what do you find so objectionable about me?"

She sniffed. "That comment, for one thing. I am not tight-assed. I'm cautious and prudent, two qualities you barely have a speaking acquaintance with."

"Is that so? Who had the birth control?"

"You *should* have had it," she said, her voice rising in anger. "You plotted to seduce me!"

"If you ask me, you didn't take a whole lot of seducing. I saw the way you looked at me when you first woke up. Can't you admit that you wanted to go out to the barn with me? Aren't you woman enough to say you wanted me as much as I wanted you?"

"Yes, I wanted you!" She gripped the frayed armrest as the truck hit another rut with more force. "But I wouldn't have if you hadn't crashed your stupid plane in the middle of the desert and thrown me totally off kilter!"

"Well, pardon me all to hell!"

"And stop hitting those ruts on purpose, dammit!"

In answer he drove straight toward a large rut and hit it so hard she thought the springs must surely have pierced a hole in her backside. Her only satisfaction was the knowledge that his seat was as bad as hers.

"Let me out," she said through clenched teeth. "I don't have to put up with this."

"Gladly." He screeched the truck to a halt, reached across and opened the passenger door.

6

A BLAST OF COLD AIR swept in and Adrienne's breath caught in her throat. She hadn't realized that Matt had turned on the heater in the truck's cab, making the interior of the truck toasty compared with the outside.

He glared at her. "Well?"

She wrapped her blanket around her and glanced into the frigid blackness. She could freeze to death trying to walk the rest of the way dressed in a blouse, skirt and moccasins. Her outburst had been imprudent, and she'd recently proclaimed herself to be the exact opposite. This man brought out such conflicting emotions in her that she couldn't think straight.

Matt leaned over and slammed the door shut again. "I didn't think you'd do it." He stepped on the gas, but she noticed that he carefully avoided the next rut.

She stared straight ahead for a long time. "Would you have let me get out?" she asked finally.

He made an impatient noise deep in his throat. "You are something else."

"Well, would you?"

He glanced at her. "You tell me. You're such an expert on my character."

"I don't think you would have. One thing you've done consistently is try to keep me safe, like Beverly said you would."

"Bev told you I'd do that?"

"Yes, and she was right. I appreciate your concern for me, Matt."

"Sure, you do."

"No, I do," she insisted. "It's just that we look at the world differently, that's all. You said it yourself tonight, when we were still in the rain and you kidded me about not enjoying sinful pleasures. You're right, I don't believe in them. I've seen what happened to my sisters' lives. The price one pays for pleasure is too high."

"And I think you talk too much," he said. "Let's drop it, okay? We're not right for each other. It's a good thing I kicked that gas can because then we both had a chance to come to our senses."

"That's right." She glanced at him and could see the tight lines of anger around his mouth. Of course he was right, so why did she feel so bereft? He'd only repeated what she'd been trying to say.

Now that they both understood the way things were, they could forget this incident and part with reasonable politeness. She'd acted maturely and cautiously by shutting down his ardor. She should be proud of herself. All the rest of the long, silent ride to town she searched for that sense of pride.

At last a sprinkling of lights appeared in the distance.

"Do you think that's it?" she asked. Her throat felt rusty.

"Yep."

"Doesn't look very big."

"Nope."

"But they should have a telephone, don't you think?"

"Yep."

"Honestly, Matt, you sound like Clint Eastwood. I'm sorry this isn't working out between us, but can't we at least have a normal conversation?"

"Nope."

Adrienne sighed. "Just because I won't go to bed with you again, you—"

"Hold it right there. Going to bed with me *isn't* the issue. Passing premature judgment on my character *is*. You've let this business with your sisters and their divorces turn you into a prissy woman with a computerized list of requirements for a partner. I resent your holding me up to some measuring stick and finding me wanting."

He hadn't shouted at her this time, but the words cut deeper than if he had. Prissy. She didn't like the sound of that. Maybe she had judged him prematurely, but everything had moved so fast, that she'd had to judge quickly or not at all. One minute she barely knew him; the next she had to decide whether they should become lovers.

She cleared her throat. "Maybe I should ask . . . why you wanted to make love to me?"

"Because I thought you had courage. I admire that. It seems I was wrong."

"Courage? Me? I'm the one who was afraid to go up in the plane, who has a fear of heights, who—"

"Who went up in the plane anyway, who set off alone in the rain to find a road, who would have dared to cross a flooded wash in her high heels to get to the other side." He glanced at her. "And was willing to tell a complete stranger that his pants were coming apart."

She stared at him. He'd painted a picture of a woman she didn't recognize, yet she'd done all those things. He was confusing her, making her doubt everything she'd always taken for granted about herself.

"There's a pay phone beside that bar," he said. "If for some reason that phone's out, the bar looks like it's still open. We can go in there."

"Okay." Adrienne noticed that the ride had smoothed out. They'd hit the main street of Saddlehorn, which was paved, but had no curbs. On her left was a closed gas station, and a string of three storefronts housing a beauty shop, a barber and a drugstore.

On the right side of the street was a market, also closed, and a bar with a curved red neon arrow flashing on and off as it pointed to a battered wooden door. Country music blared loud enough from within to be heard through the closed door. Two pickups in similar condition to Archie's were parked in front of the bar.

On either side of the main street, porch lights gleamed from the houses scattered down the unpaved side roads. If necessary, Adrienne would knock on every door until she found a working phone. It occurred to her that knocking on strange doors at four in the morning was not the action of a cautious, prudent stockbroker. No wonder Matt saw her differently than she saw herself, but this weekend was so atypical of her life that he'd been fooled into imagining she was like this all the time.

Matt parked the truck beside the telephone booth, the only shiny, modern-looking structure in Saddlehorn. Adrienne opened the truck door and started to get out.

"Need some change?" Matt asked.

She'd forgotten she didn't have money, didn't have her telephone credit card, didn't have any way of using this telephone. "Please, if you have some," she said, chastened. Once again he'd saved her.

Matt raised his hips from the seat and dug in his pocket. "Two quarters, a nickel and some pennies," he said, sorting through the coins in his palm. "You'd better call collect."

"I will." She accepted the quarter he handed her. "Thank you."

"Better wait and thank me after you find out if the phone works. Otherwise we'll have to go in there," he added, inclining his head toward the bar, "and it sounds like there's a rowdy bunch inside."

"Right." Holding the blanket around her, Adrienne hopped down to the ground. She hoped they wouldn't have to enter the noisy bar. Along with the music, occasional loud comments from belligerent-sounding men burst into the night. No doubt everyone in the bar was tanked up, as Archie had been when he'd driven home from here. Adrienne supposed she and Matt were lucky Archie had decided to go home. He could have stayed with the men still drinking at the bar.

She closed the phone booth door and picked up the receiver as she put the quarter in the slot. When she heard a dial tone, she wanted to shout with joy, but she kept silent, not wanting to call attention to herself and Matt. She punched in the area code of her parents' number with trembling fingers. Finally she'd be able to talk to them, to find out about Granny, to—

Matt yelled and Adrienne whirled toward the truck in time to see two burly men wearing cowboy hats yank Matt from the cab as he fought to ward them off. She dropped the receiver and threw open the door. The blanket fell to the ground as she ran.

"What do you think you're doing?" she cried, rounding the front of the truck and grabbing the first man's arm in both hands. She smelled alcohol on his breath. "Leave him alone!"

"Butt out, lady." The man thrust her away with one arm as he grappled with Matt, who was swearing as he worked to free himself. "We got a p'tential lawbreaker, here."

"I said let him go!" Adrienne hurled herself at the man again, ripping at his sheepskin jacket and dislodging his hat. "He hasn't done anything wrong!"

"Got Archie's pickup," the man grunted. Underneath the hat he was nearly bald. "Got Archie's clothes." He shrugged her away again. "Grab his other arm, Jeb. I got ahold of this one."

"You don't understand," Adrienne pleaded, deciding to try reason since she was no physical match for either man. "Archie loaned us these clothes."

"Us?" The man pinned Matt's arm behind his back and turned to glance at her. "Damnation, you got on Dorothy's duds. Can you hold him, Jeb? I'd better corral this little gal."

"Don't you touch her," Matt warned in a low voice.

"You quit strugglin' and we won't," the man named Jeb said. "Right, Curtis?"

Curtis picked up his hat and dusted it off before replacing it on his head. Then he adjusted the collar of his sheepskin coat and eyed Matt and Adrienne. "I don't trust neither of 'em."

"Look, I'll stand here quietly," Matt said. "Just leave her alone."

A lump formed in Adrienne's throat. He was still taking care of her, in spite of all that had been said.

"Yeah, well, if you wanna stand quietly, you can do it over by Curtis's pickup," Jeb said, angling his head toward a rusty green Ford with a crumpled rear fender.

"Good idea." Curtis grabbed Adrienne's arm. "Let's go, missy."

"I said to leave her alone!" Matt said, and nearly broke away from Jeb.

Curtis released his grip on Adrienne's arm. "Jist don't try nothin' funny, then."

"I won't," Adrienne replied. "Listen, we crash-landed a plane out on the mesa and walked to the road, where Archie picked us up, but his phone didn't work, so we drove into town so we could call my parents. If you'll let me call them, you can talk to them. They'll verify my story."

"How do we know who you're callin', missy?" Curtis said. "Could be another one of yer gang."

"Gang?" Adrienne said. "For heaven's sake. We're not a gang, we're—"

Curtis snorted. "You say Archie let you have Bessie?"

"Who?"

"His truck, missy. Archie let you borrow it?"

"Well, sort of. He'd told us he was out of gas and he was asleep when we found the gas can, but I'm sure he would have wanted us to get to a phone."

Curtis snorted again. "In a pig's eye. Archie don't never loan out his pickup."

"Hey, Curtis," Jeb called as they reached the side of the banged-up vehicle. "Fetch that little item outa the truck, will ya? I got my hands full."

"I'll git it. Knew that's what you wanted," Curtis said, opening the door.

The overhead light in the truck's cab didn't work, so Adrienne couldn't see what Curtis was after until he backed out of the truck and turned with a double-barreled shotgun pointed right at them.

"You sonofabitch," Matt swore softly. "Put that damn thing away before somebody gets hurt."

Jeb released Matt's arms and went over to stand beside Curtis. "Way I figure it, maybe somebody's already hurt." He wiped his large nose on the sleeve of his denim jacket. "What'd you do with Archie?"

"Archie's fine," Matt said. "Drunk but fine. I tried to wake him up before we left with the truck, but I couldn't do it. After a fifth of booze he was out."

"Yeah, sure," Jeb said. "You knocked him out, that's what. Or worse. Curtis is right. Archie don't let nobody drive that truck."

"Yeah, and lookit this one in Dorothy's best duds," Curtis said, waving the shotgun in Adrienne's direction.

"Will you put that damn thing away?" Matt shouted.

Curtis ignored him. "You picture Archie loanin' out Dorothy's best duds, Jeb?"

"On Judgment Day, maybe. He 'bout built a shrine to that woman."

Adrienne noticed that the two men were weaving slightly. They were nearly as drunk as Archie had been when she and Matt had stopped him on the road. She had an idea. "This is just a big misunderstanding," she said. "We can straighten everything out if we all just sit down and have a long talk. It's mighty cold out here," she added, throwing in the folksy word *mighty* for extra effect. "How about if we all go inside and have a drink together, my treat? I'm sure we can take care of everything."

Matt raised one eyebrow at her but she smiled back, as if she had everything under control.

Curtis glanced at Jeb. "It *is* damned cold out here, Jeb."

"Shut up, Curtis. She's tryin' to trick us."

"How?"

"I'm not sure. Jist think she is. She may be dressed country, but she looks like one of them sneaky city women t'me."

Curtis waggled the shotgun. "So what'dya think we should do with 'em, Jeb?"

Jeb took off his hat and scratched his head of gray, bristly hair. "Search 'em," he said, and clapped his hat back on his head. "You keep that gun trained on 'em real good, Curtis. I'll search 'em." He walked over to Matt. "Put your hands in the air."

"No fair," Curtis complained as Jeb patted Matt down. "I wanna search the girl."

Jeb chuckled. "You would. You ain't had much fun since Francine left, have you?"

Adrienne's skin prickled. Now she feared for more than her life. She glanced at Matt and her eyes widened at the predatory expression in his eyes.

"You do one thing to that woman," Matt said, his tone deceptively calm as he gazed at Curtis, "and I'll turn you from a bass into a soprano, so help me God."

Curtis sneered at him. "You fergit, I got the gun."

"Makes no difference," Matt said.

Adrienne couldn't imagine how he could manage against a shotgun, but something about his manner convinced her he would.

He must have convinced Curtis, too, because the man shrugged and looked away. "She ain't my type, anyways," he said.

"That's for damn sure," Matt said, and as Adrienne watched in amazement, he winked at her.

For no earthly reason, she regained hope that they'd get out of their predicament. They were still in the same mess, but Matt's wink told her he hadn't lost his cool. If Matt still believed they'd be okay, she could believe it, too.

Jeb approached her. She tensed, wondering if he was any better than Curtis. He glanced at her, reddened and walked away. "She ain't hiding nothin'," he told Curtis.

"You didn't look!" Curtis exclaimed.

"Don't feel right, searchin' a woman."

Curtis snorted. "You're chicken, that's what you are."

"Watch yerself, Curtis." Jeb glared at the man holding the gun.

"Aw, you know I didn't mean nothin'."

"Jist watch yerself."

"Didn't mean nothin'," Curtis mumbled again. Then he waved the gun. "What're we gonna do with 'em?"

Jeb rubbed his chin and made a scratching sound against the stubble. "Take 'em back to Archie's. We'll make 'em tell what they done to him."

Adrienne's hopes took a downward turn. "Let me call my parents," she said. "You can stand right there. You can listen in. Just let me tell them I'm okay." She wondered now if that was the truth, but she had to call, had to end their worry that she was dead or missing.

"We ain't wastin' no time on telephone calls," Jeb said.

"Five minutes won't make that much difference," Matt said. "Let her call."

"Nope," Jeb said. "We're leavin' for Archie's now."

"Archie's truck's out of gas," Matt said. "We barely had enough to make it here. And the gas station's closed."

Jeb scratched his chin. "You're prob'ly right about the gas. Archie ain't never got enough gas in that blamed truck. Curtis, keep that gun on both of 'em while I siphon some gas off'n yer tank."

"You gonna pay me back for the gas, Jeb?"

"Yeah, yeah. Jist watch 'em, okay?" He walked toward Archie's truck.

"Couldn't I use this time to call my parents?" Adrienne asked.

"Nope," Curtis replied, wagging his head from side to side. "Jeb says no, and that means no."

"But I—"

"Shut your mouth, before I shut it for you."

Matt stepped forward. "Watch how you talk to her."

"You wanna make somethin' of it?" Curtis pointed the gun at Matt's chest.

"Let it go," Adrienne murmured. "No use getting shot over bad manners."

Matt glanced at her. "The way you said it, it sounded like you cared about me a little."

"Of course I care about you," she flung back. "I just—"

"Just what?" he asked softly, holding her gaze.

Jeb's abrupt return ended the moment. "That takes care of the gas," he said, wiping his hands on his pants. "Curtis, give me the gun and you take the girl in your truck. This other one can drive Bessie. I'll hold the gun on him to make sure he don't do nothin'."

"Wait a minute," Matt objected. "I'll go with Curtis. You take her," he said, pointing to Adrienne.

"Ain't nobody drivin' my truck but me," Curtis said. "And I can't drive and hold a gun on him."

"Yeah, I know," Jeb said, rubbing his chin again. "Nope, gotta be the way I said first off."

"The hell it does." Matt flexed his hands and rose on the balls of his feet.

Jeb lifted the shotgun from Curtis's arms and pointed it at Matt. "You wanna argue? I can always jist shoot you, say you were tryin' to git away after stealin' Archie's truck. Any way you look at it, you didn't have no permission fer that truck. And I don't like you much. Be a lot less trouble to shoot you and leave you here."

Fear stabbed through Adrienne. She had no idea what these half-drunk men might do. The thought of something happening to Matt made her stomach churn.

"He's right, Matt," she said. "We have no proof Archie wanted us to take the truck. Don't do anything silly."

"Best listen to the lady," Jeb said. "You ain't got much choice, mister. Now go git in Archie's truck."

Adrienne watched Matt walk back to Archie's truck and climb in. Jeb followed with the gun pointed at Matt.

"I dropped Archie's blanket on the ground," she called after them. "It's there by the truck." She had one last hope that Jeb would go after the blanket and Matt would get away, but instead Jeb ordered Matt out of the truck again and had him retrieve the blanket.

"Time to take a drive, missy," Curtis said, leering at her.

"We'll lead," Jeb said, putting the blanket on the seat next to Matt as he climbed in on the passenger side of Archie's truck. Jeb held the gun ready across his lap, the muzzle two inches from Matt's groin.

"The road's bumpy," Matt said, turning the key in the ignition. "That thing could go off."

"Wouldn't that be too bad," Jeb said. "You bein' such a stud and all."

Matt grimaced. "I don't suppose you'd take my word that I won't try anything if you'd point that somewhere else."

"Nope."

"Didn't think so." Matt turned the truck around slowly, glancing all the while at Jeb's finger on the shotgun's trigger. One jolt and he'd be a eunuch. And all because he'd leaped in and offered to fly Adrienne to her parents' house. The big macho pilot to the rescue. In return he'd had the fun of a wrecked plane, some interrupted lovemaking, several fights with Adrienne, and now the possibility of this jerk shooting away the family jewels.

He drove with care down the deserted street. He didn't even want to think about the rutted road to Archie's place.

"Believe I'll have a snort," Jeb said, reaching inside his denim jacket for a flask.

"I wish you wouldn't do that when your finger's still on the trigger," Matt said.

Jeb cackled. "Make you nervous?"

"I'd like to see you drive down a road with some trigger-happy sonofabitch pointing a shotgun at your pride and joy," Matt muttered.

Jeb took a swig from his flask. "Shoulda thoughta that before you stole this truck."

"I didn't steal it," Matt said, gritting his teeth. He prayed Archie would remember him and Adrienne when they got back to the cabin. Archie might have been in such an alcoholic fog the past few hours that he wouldn't recall picking up two bedraggled people on the road and loaning them his clothes. And of course Adrienne was right; technically Archie hadn't loaned them the truck, so even if he'd found Matt's note he might be upset that they'd taken it.

"So what's yer racket?" Jeb asked. "I been thinkin' about the airplane. You fly in someplace and take what you want? That it?"

"No."

"Used to be rumors that Archie and Dorothy had a stash of gold. You hear about that?"

"No." Matt glanced in the rearview mirror. He'd keep an eye on Curtis. If the guy started bothering Adrienne, he'd have to do something.

"Won't talk, huh?" Jeb said, and took another noisy drink from his flask. "Don't matter. If we find you done somethin' to Archie, we'll make you talk. Won't bother with no sheriff right away, neither."

Sweat dampened Matt's forehead. He accelerated slightly, found a smooth stretch of road and took the opportunity to check his rearview mirror again. Fortunately, Curtis didn't seem to be bothering Adrienne, who was huddled against the passenger door. Matt took the road as slowly as he dared.

The sky was lightening by the time they pulled through the break in Archie's fence and drove toward the house. Matt felt as if he'd aged twenty years in the past few hours. Maybe at last the nightmare would be over. As long as Archie corroborated the story Matt and Adrienne had told, then these two trigger-happy hotheads would be on their way. After the sun came up, Archie's telephone wires would dry and Adrienne could call her parents.

He parked the truck in the same spot where Archie had left it. Curtis pulled the other pickup in behind him.

"Git out slow," Jeb said, training the gun on him. "And don't try runnin'. I might miss you, but I'd pick off yer girlfriend."

"I won't run. I have no reason to. Archie will set you guys straight, and then I'll never have to see your ugly mugs again." Matt eased himself stiffly to the ground. Thirty miles of driving with most of his muscles tensed had left him sore and hobbling as he moved around to the front of the truck.

Adrienne got out and hurried over to him, with Curtis swearing at her to slow down. "Are you okay?"

He gave her a lopsided grin. "In a manner of speaking. I'm still in one piece."

"I was so afraid he'd fall asleep and accidentally pull the trigger," Adrienne said, glancing several feet away to where Jeb stood in the gray of early morning.

"I had a small concern about that myself." He noticed her shiver. "Let's go inside."

Matt made sure Adrienne walked in front of him in case Jeb tripped and discharged the shotgun into their backs by accident. Together they tromped across the narrow porch and in through the unlocked door.

Once inside, Curtis began calling Archie's name.

"He's probably still in his easy chair by the fire, where we left him," Matt said. Adrienne and Curtis continued to block his view of the room.

"No, he ain't," Curtis said.

"Then maybe he went to bed," Adrienne suggested, turning toward the bedroom.

"You stay here," Jeb said. "Curtis, you look in the bedroom, and the bathroom, too."

In a moment Curtis returned. "He ain't there."

"The barn, then," Matt said, as panic got a toehold inside him. Where was the old galoot?

Jeb motioned Curtis to the door. "Check the barn."

"I'll bet that's where he is," Adrienne said after Curtis left. "Remember, Matt? He was having that burro delivered today, and he probably wanted to check the stall and make sure everything was ready."

"That's probably where he is, then, checking the stall." Matt looked at her and wondered if she was thinking what he was, about what they'd done in the barn a few hours ago. Her cheeks tinged a faint pink, and she glanced away, so maybe she had thought of it.

Holding her and kissing her soft skin had been the only saving grace in one of the worst nights of his life. He wouldn't mind repeating that part, but she'd made herself pretty clear on that score. She wanted a no-risk relationship, and she didn't see that as a possibility with him. Which it wasn't.

Curtis came back through the door. He was puffing. "I looked all over tarnation, in the barn, around the side of the house, ever'where. He ain't nowheres, Jeb." He braced his feet apart and stared at Matt and Adrienne. "What I think is, them two done something to Archie, jist like we was afeared of."

7

ADRIENNE SWALLOWED and glanced at Matt. "I'm sure there's some explanation," she said. "Maybe a friend came over and—"

"No use makin' up lies," Jeb said. "Curtis is right. What we gotta do now is search some more, fer where you mighta hid the body."

"The body?" Matt protested. "Come on, you guys. You've been watching too many reruns of *Magnum*. We didn't harm a single gray hair on Archie's head."

"He was asleep in the chair when we left," Adrienne said.

"Then why ain't he here?" Curtis asked.

"I don't know." Adrienne glanced around the room, as if he could be hidden somewhere and they'd missed him in the dim predawn light filtering through the windows.

"There's stories," Jeb said, "about cuttin' folks up after doin' away with them. Maybe that's what they done. Check the bathtub for blood."

Curtis walked back to the bedroom.

"This is stupid," Matt said. "Do we look the kind of people who would kill an old man and dismember his corpse?"

Jeb gazed at him. "Shore do."

Matt snorted and shook his head. "Okay, so we look like desperate criminals. But why? Why would we kill Archie?"

"Fer his gold."

"We don't know anything about any gold, but even if we did, why didn't we have it with us when you picked us up in town?"

"You got that hid, too, somewheres."

"Oh, for Pete's sake."

Curtis came back into the room. "Archie don't have no bathtub."

"So what took you so long?" Jeb demanded.

"I was lookin'. Didn't find no blood in the shower, or in the sink, or in the wastebasket, or in the toilet, or—"

"All right!" Jeb approached Adrienne and pointed the gun at her. "You gonna tell us what you done with him?"

She was sick of dealing with these two with their blessed gun and their grisly theories. Weariness claimed every muscle in her body and she could no longer tolerate this nonsense. She pushed the cold muzzle of the gun away. "We don't know where he is."

"Adrienne," Matt warned, "be care—"

"I'm tired," she interrupted. "And these idiots keep asking the same dumb question about what we supposedly did to Archie. I've had it. We don't know where he is," she said, facing Jeb. "Can't you get that through your thick heads? We don't know!"

Jeb stepped back, but he brought the gun up again immediately. "Git some rope from the barn," he said to Curtis.

Adrienne's exhaustion vanished. "A rope?" Her throat constricted as if she could feel the rope tightening around her neck in an old-fashioned lynching, just like she'd seen in the movies. "Now, look here, you have no proof of anything, and frontier justice is a thing of the past. Besides, you'd go to jail, maybe even the electric chair if you string us up without a trial."

Jeb regarded her without smiling. "I was fixin' to tie you up," he said, "not string you up. So Curtis kin guard you while I look around," Jeb added.

Adrienne's relief disappeared as she imagined herself and Matt tied up inside the cabin with Curtis, who hated Matt and lusted after her.

Matt cleared his throat. "I wouldn't trust Curtis to guard us, if I were you."

"Curtis kin guard jist fine. I'm not shore he kin search so good, so I'm doin' that."

"Guarding takes more intelligence than searching," Matt said, "and anyone can see that you're a lot smarter than Curtis. If it were me, I'd let Curtis wear himself out looking all around the place. I'd keep the important job of guarding the prisoners for myself. We might be able to talk Curtis into letting us get away, but we'd never be able to pull that on you."

Jeb appeared pleased with the assessment. "That's right. Can't fool me."

"Then you'll send Curtis out to search," Matt said.

Adrienne held her breath.

"Nope," Jeb replied. "I'll jist lecture him on the subject of not lettin' you git away. Curtis listens to me."

Adrienne exchanged a glance with Matt. "I can't imagine where Archie is," she said, and heard the note of despair in her voice.

"He'll be along," Matt said softly. "Don't worry."

Adrienne gazed at him. The harsh words she'd spoken in the truck, when she'd told him that he was unacceptable as a potential partner, came back to mock her. Unacceptable? All through this long night he'd done nothing but keep her from harm and bolster her spirits. In a situation like this Alex would have folded a long time ago.

Something else occurred to her. Perhaps this night, complete with the loss of his airplane, had taught Matt a few things. Maybe after tonight he would change; he couldn't possibly remain the same cocky, impulsive person after this experience. She began to wonder seriously if she should give him another chance, assuming he'd even want one; he might not after the way she'd spoken to him.

Curtis came through the door loaded down with ropes. "Found a whole bunch," he announced. "From Archie's mining stuff, y'know."

"Good," Jeb said. "Git two chairs from the kitchen."

Curtis dropped the ropes in a dusty pile and left for the kitchen. He returned carrying two old ladder-back chairs.

"One here," Jeb said, pointing to one side of the living room, "and the other one there. Facing each other."

"Wouldn't it be easier to guard us if we were in the same place?" Matt asked.

Adrienne knew he'd seen the same movie scenes she had, where the two prisoners managed to scoot their chairs close enough to untie each other.

Jeb waved the gun at him. "Why don't you jist shut up? I'm tired of yer advice." He pointed at the kitchen chair Curtis had placed in front of the room's largest window. "Sit." When Matt hesitated, Jeb leveled the gun at his chest. "Sit."

Matt shrugged. "Okay, if you're going to be that way about it."

"Tie him up first," Jeb ordered, and Curtis gathered a length of rope and approached Matt.

Jeb pointed at Adrienne. "You sit there," he said, indicating the ladder-back chair in front of the bookshelves.

Adrienne sat on the wooden seat and watched as Curtis tied Matt's hands behind the chair on the opposite side of the room. Matt said something to him she couldn't hear and Curtis nodded. Then he wound a second rope around Matt's legs and the chair legs. The ropes looked painfully tight, but Matt didn't wince. He gazed at her as if he were sitting on a park bench contemplating a scenic view.

Then Curtis approached her with two more lengths of rope, and Matt's expression changed. His jaw tightened and his eyes narrowed as Curtis tied her arms behind her chair. The position thrust her breasts forward against the eyelet blouse, and when Curtis came around in front of her to tie her legs, his leer told her that he'd noticed, too.

Curtis managed to touch her calves more than was necessary as he tied her legs to the chair, and Adrienne noticed Matt straining against his ropes for the first time. Finally Curtis finished and moved away.

"I'm leavin' to search," Jeb announced, and walked out the front door without a backward glance.

Curtis looked at each of them in turn. Then he rocked on the balls of his feet and puffed out his chest. "Now *I'm* in charge."

Matt returned his gaze. "How nice for you."

"Yep. Nice." Curtis swung his attention back to Adrienne. "Very nice," he said, his tone changing.

"Don't even think it," Matt said.

"You ain't in no spot to tell me what to do, neither." Curtis ignored Matt and walked over to Adrienne.

She turned her head away as he stared at her breasts. A humming noise started up in the kitchen, and she looked in that direction, hoping for somebody, or something, to save her. Then she realized that the hum came from the refrigerator. The electricity was back on. The phone lines might be dry, too, except that she couldn't get to them.

Curtis leaned down, and she smelled a combination of beer, sweat and mud. He fingered the top button of her blouse. "You sure are a pretty little lady."

The door flew open and Archie charged into the room, his gray hair on end, his eyes wild. "What in tarnation's goin' on?"

Adrienne sank back against the chair. "Thank God you're here, Archie. These lunatics thought we'd killed you."

"I only see one lunatic, and he's done hog-tied my friends," Archie said. "Close yer mouth and put down the dang gun, Curtis, and let's get these people un-hooked from the chairs."

Curtis laid the gun on the coffee table and looked sheepish as he walked over toward Matt's chair. "Jeb and me thought you was dead," he explained as he worked on Matt's ropes. "We seen these two in town with yer truck and wearin' yer clothes. We brung 'em back here and you was gone. We thought they'd chopped you up in the bathtub."

"Don't have no bathtub." Archie fumbled with the knots at Adrienne's wrists and muttered to himself.

"I know," Curtis said.

"Where's Jeb?"

"Out lookin' fer yer remains."

Archie muttered some more, and Adrienne caught a few phrases about "dang fools," and "crazy idiots." When her wrists were free, she shook her hands to restore feeling in her fingers. Then she examined her wrists where the skin had been rubbed raw.

"I kin git you some ointment fer that," Archie said, bending down to untie the rope around her legs. "That is, right after I knock some sense into that fool Curtis."

"It's okay, Archie. Just tell them we didn't steal your truck or your clothes, so they'll go away. I don't want you to fight him."

Archie removed the rope from around her legs and looked again at her wrists. He swore, and then apologized. "Can't abide somebody abusin' a woman," he said, and stood up to face Curtis. "Yer a fool, Curtis, and so's Jeb. This nice young couple crashed their airplane near here and needed a little hosp'talty. Which I was in the business of providin', until you trussed 'em up like turkeys."

"An airplane crash? They was tellin' the truth about that?" Curtis asked, his eyes brightening. "Where is it? Maybe we could help haul it out fer them."

"Dunno where it is," Archie said, "but no need of you messin' with it."

"Maybe they could help," Matt said casually, pausing on his way over to see how Adrienne was.

She stared at him. Surely he wouldn't want to involve Jeb and Curtis in the possible recovery of his airplane. Besides, his wallet and her purse were still in the plane, assuming it could be reached. She didn't trust Jeb and Curtis not to steal whatever they could. "Matt—" she began, but he glanced over and motioned her to silence. She kept quiet. After all he'd done, she'd have to trust him.

He gave the approximate location of the plane while Archie stood next to him shaking his head in disapproval. Curtis left soon after that, saying he'd find Jeb and they'd set out to look for the plane very soon.

"I wouldn'ta told him that," Archie said as soon as Curtis left.

"I don't know why you did," Adrienne added.

Matt turned to her. "I didn't. I gave them a fake location. Otherwise they might have accidentally found it, but where I told them to look they'll be rummaging around all day for nothing."

Archie's eyes sparkled. "Good fer you. Them two deserve it, after what they done." He motioned to Adrienne. "Markin' up her wrists with that rope. Let me git some ointment."

"First I want to try the phone," Adrienne said, crossing the room. "If the electricity's back on, maybe the phone lines are dry."

"Shore thing. Should be," Archie said. "And I gotta reset that danged ugly clock."

Adrienne glanced up at the clock hanging over the bookshelf. Archie was right; it was ugly. The clock face was surrounded by a molded plastic still life of a basketed wine bottle, a cluster of purple grapes and wedges of cheese in a shade of yellow she'd never seen in nature. As Adrienne picked up the telephone receiver, Archie grabbed one of the ladder-back chairs and climbed up to adjust the hands on the clock. Then Adrienne realized she was listening to a dial tone, and she lost track of everything else around her.

She called collect. The old rotary dial seemed to take forever, but at last the operator answered and Adrienne gave her the information for the call. Finally she heard the phone ringing at her parents' house. She closed her eyes in relief.

"Hello?" Her father's deep baritone answered quickly, with an urgency that told her he'd been pacing by the phone.

"Dad, it's—"

The operator interrupted. "I have a collect call for anyone from Adrienne Burnham. Will you accept the charges?"

"God, yes!" her father exploded. "Adrienne?"

"I'm fine, Dad. Just fine."

He expelled a breath. "Thank the Lord. Just a minute. I'll get your mother."

Adrienne thought she might cry. She bit her lip and swiped at her eyes.

In a moment her mother came on the extension. "You're okay?"

"I'm fine," Adrienne said, fighting back tears at hearing their voices so full of concern. She didn't want them to think she was upset. Later she'd tell them the whole story, but she wasn't up to it now. "We had some trouble with the plane, and I couldn't get to a phone."

"Where are you?" her father asked.

Adrienne thought quickly of how much she should tell them. "In Saddlehorn, Arizona."

"Never heard of the place," he said. "Do you need me to drive down and pick you up?"

"No, no. It's too far. You'd just get me up there and I'd have to turn around and come back to Tucson for work on Monday."

"Oh, honey," her mother said, emotion choking her voice. "We were so worried. The authorities said they couldn't start the search until dawn, so we've been up all night, waiting and praying. I'm so glad..." She stopped speaking, and Adrienne knew she was trying to gain control of her tears.

Adrienne swallowed the lump in her throat. "I'm sorry you had to worry. And you know how much I wanted to be there. Is Granny...is she—?"

"She died about four this morning," her father said gently. "Real peaceful."

"Oh." Tears dribbled down Adrienne's cheeks, despite her efforts not to cry. "I should have been there, Dad."

"I know you wanted to be, sweetheart, but things don't always work out. At least you're all right. That's the most important thing."

"Yes, but I wanted to see her one last time."

"I know," he soothed.

"We stayed with her, honey," her mother said. "We took a portable phone down to the barn, in case we heard from you, and we stayed with her until she died."

"Thanks, Mom." Adrienne choked back a sob. "Well, I suppose I'd better go. Matt and I have some things to take care of before we can leave." Her sobs threatened to change into hysterical laughter. They certainly did have a few things to take care of. All their money and identification was somewhere at the bottom of a canyon. Yet, if she told her father, he'd break speed limits to get down here, and she didn't want him to do that. She could work herself out of this, now that the telephone was in order again.

"I'm assuming the plane malfunctioned and you had to land at Saddlehorn," her father said.

Adrienne barely hesitated. "That's right."

"Can you get it fixed?"

Again the laughter pushed upward from her chest. "I'm not sure," she said, "but if not, I'm sure buses are available. We'll be fine."

"Call me if you run into any snags," her father said.

"Of course."

"We love you, sweetheart," her mother said.

"I love you both, too." Adrienne knew she had to hang up or they'd hear her voice breaking. "Goodbye for now. I'll be in touch." Their goodbyes drifted up to her as she lowered the receiver to its cradle. Then she put her face in her hands to muffle the sound of her crying.

Within seconds she felt an arm around her shoulder. Matt turned her carefully around and guided her into his arms, where she sobbed out her grief and soaked the black western shirt. At last, exhausted, she subsided into snuffles. She heard Archie offer to fetch the box of tissues. She needed to blow her nose, but hated to leave the warm comfort of Matt's arms. For a moment longer she enjoyed the solid security of his embrace, but when she heard Archie's returning footsteps, she backed away.

"Your granny died, didn't she?" Matt asked softly.

Adrienne nodded and reached for the tissue sticking up from the box Archie thrust forward. She blew her nose and wiped her eyes. "At four this morning," she said, gazing up at him.

"I'm sorry."

"Me, too," Archie said.

"I suppose we need to get you on a bus or something, whatever runs through Saddlehorn, so you can be up there in time for the funeral."

Adrienne stared at him. He wasn't making sense. "What funeral?"

He looked puzzled. "Oh. Well, maybe your family doesn't believe in funerals. I hadn't thought of that."

"I don't know very many people who have funerals for a horse," Adrienne said, still confused. "Although in Granny's case, I wouldn't mind. But it would be too much trouble and expense to expect that my parents—"

"Hold it." Matt's eyes narrowed. "Did you say *horse?*"

8

ADRIENNE COULDN'T understand Matt's agitation. "Yes, I said 'horse,' *h-o-r-s-e*. Why?"

"You're telling me that Granny was not your grandmother, but was, in fact, a *horse?*"

"Of course she is—was—a horse. I told you that."

"No, you didn't."

Adrienne objected to both the set of his jaw and the glower in his eyes. "I must have. You probably weren't listening."

Matt was shouting now. "You mean to tell me," he said, pointing a finger at her, "that I have wrecked my plane, risked my life and nearly had my vital parts blown away all for a damned *horse?*"

"She's not a damned horse!" Adrienne knocked his accusing finger away. "She happens to be—or was—my best friend!"

"Then why didn't you call her Flicka or Trigger or something like that? Who on God's green earth names a horse *Granny?*"

"Now, Matt," Archie began. "Names of animals is kinda personal. No need to git riled."

"I think there's a tremendous need to get riled," Matt said, including Archie in his glare. "She names this animal Granny, which everybody knows is what you call your grandmother, not your horse, and then she goes around talking about the fact that Granny is dying and she has to be with her. What would *you* think?"

"Well, now, I reckon—"

"I'll tell you why I called her Granny." Adrienne put her hands on her hips. "Because she was already twelve when I got her, and she *was* a grandmother. So there."

"Brilliant. Now if you could have explained that to me while we were still at Bev's house, maybe all this wouldn't have happened."

"Because you wouldn't have flown me just to take care of a dying horse, is that it?"

"I don't know, but I deserved to be told what the stakes were!"

"Which for me, were damned high! Not that I expect somebody who worships cold, inanimate objects like airplanes to understand what a loving, wonderful, dear . . . soft . . ." She started to cry again in great, hiccuping gulps.

"Aw, hell."

"I got an idea," Archie said, putting down the tissue box. "You two been through a heck of a lot, and it's makin' you act like you ain't too growed up. Before you tear each other to bits, maybe you oughta git some sleep."

"Not . . . in the . . . same room with him, I'm not," Adrienne said between sobs. She grabbed at another tissue and blew her nose.

"Then you take the bed and he'll take the barn," Archie said. "Dorothy don't arrive fer another few hours yet."

Adrienne wiped her nose. "Dorothy? Your wife?"

"My burro," Archie replied. "Dorothy the third."

"Oh. That's right."

"So off with both of you. Everythin' will look better after some shut-eye."

"Which reminds me," Matt said. "Where were you when we came back with Jeb and Curtis? When we left, you were sawing logs in that chair over there."

"I was visitin' Dorothy."

"Your burro?" Matt asked.

"My ornery wife."

"But I thought she died?"

"She's in the ground, if that's what you mean. Over on a little rise 'bout a mile from here. We watch the sun come up every mornin', Dorothy and me. Sometimes we talk. Sometimes we don't."

Touched by the admission, Adrienne gazed at the old man. "I think that's sweet," she said.

"It may be sweet, but it damn near got us killed," Matt said.

Adrienne glared at him. "I wouldn't expect you to understand Archie and Dorothy's relationship, either," she said, and flounced off toward Archie's bedroom.

"At least they're two people," Matt called after her. "One of them doesn't have four legs and a tail!"

"Now, now," Archie said. "You git on out to the barn. I'll git you a blanket. You kin lie on a fresh bed of straw. Bein' a city boy, bet you ain't never done that."

Adrienne paused to hear Matt's reply.

"Once," he said, "but it wasn't much fun."

"That's for sure!" she called out and slammed the bedroom door.

ADRIENNE AWOKE and lay beneath the patchwork quilt trying to get her bearings. Gradually she remembered where she was, but she had no idea how long she'd slept. She remembered stretching out on Dorothy's rose-colored spread, but the quilt now keeping her warm had been folded at the foot of the bed earlier, when she'd fallen instantly asleep. Archie must have covered her.

The house was quiet as she slipped her feet back into Dorothy's moccasins and opened the bedroom door. She crept into the living room and consulted the ugly plastic clock. Three-fifteen in the afternoon. Sun streamed in through the windows. Adrienne noticed that the empty whisky bottle was gone from beside the easy chair and the fireplace had been swept out.

The old newspapers still rested on the coffee table, but they'd been adjusted so they lay in a neat pile. Adrienne finally understood about the newspapers. Archie didn't read them, or books, either, for that matter. Dorothy had, and these were the last newspapers she'd read or done the crosswords in before she died.

Adrienne looked down at the clothes she wore, Dorothy's clothes. She marveled that Archie had loaned them to her, considering the reverence in which he held his late wife. Outfitting Matt was one thing, but allowing Adrienne to wear Dorothy's clothes was entirely different.

Thinking of Matt reminded her of their last fight. She tried to remember if she'd mentioned at Beverly's that Granny was a horse. Surely she'd told him. But then again, the incident with his splitting pants, the revelation that Beverly had planned for them to meet and the unexpected phone call about Granny had rattled her more than a little. She might have forgotten to explain who, or what, Granny was.

If so, did Matt have the right to be angry? Adrienne thought of all he'd suffered, none of which he had deserved. His only real crime was not insuring his plane properly, but adequate insurance wouldn't have changed the course of events. Matt still would have been forced to hike through the rain, ride with a drunken old man, confront two belligerent rednecks, be threatened with a shotgun, and be tied up.

He'd endured it all with an amazing degree of grace, considering that Adrienne had rejected him sexually and informed him he was too impulsive and disorganized to suit her. Then, as a final blow, he'd learned that they'd been racing to the bedside of a dying horse, not a dying grandmother.

Adrienne felt ashamed of herself. More than that, she felt a warmth toward Matt that overrode anything she'd formerly believed about his character. Besides, as she'd considered before, this incident with his plane would certainly teach him to be more prudent. In that case, what was so wrong with Matthew Kirkland? She should be welcoming the embrace of such a man, not running away from it.

She returned to the bedroom to freshen up. A few minutes with Dorothy's comb, a bit of toothpaste rubbed across her teeth with her forefinger, some cool water splashed on her face, and she was ready to apologize to Matt. With luck he wouldn't reject her as she had him.

The mud had dried enough for Adrienne to pick her way across the dirt yard to the barn. The truck was gone, and she was pleased to think she'd be able to talk with Matt in private. The barn door was partly open and Adrienne heard the rustle of straw. The noise brought back the memory of the last time she'd heard straw rustle, as Matt was loving her. A throb of desire pulsed within her like a single drumbeat.

She opened the door and slipped inside. "Matt," she said, approaching the stall. "Are you—" She stopped as Archie, on his hands and knees spreading more straw, turned to grin at her. A chaw of tobacco swelled one cheek.

"Lookit that. Finally git up, did you?"

Adrienne nodded and tried to mask her disappointment. "Did Matt take the truck somewhere?"

"Shore did. I made him eat some peanut butter sandwiches first, though. Nothin' like peanut butter t'pick you up."

"Where did he go?" Adrienne wondered if, in his anger, he'd left her here to find her own way home.

"Back t'the canyon," Archie said, shifting the wad of tobacco. "Took some ropes, too. Gonna try gittin' down to his airplane."

"Alone?" Fear punched her in the stomach.

"Yup. Dorothy the third's comin' pretty soon, so I couldn't leave. You was dead t'the world, so he took off."

"I have to help him," Adrienne said without thinking. "Is there any way I could get out there?"

Archie stood up, took off his battered western hat and wiped his forehead with his sleeve. "Don't rightly know how. He's got the truck, and Dorothy the third's not here yet. Besides, she ain't broke to ride. I hafta work with her some. There ain't no other transportation, except . . ." He paused and spit into a galvanized pail in the corner of the stall. "Well, there's the bicycle Dorothy usta ride."

"That would do. Where is it?"

Archie looked up to the rafters of the barn and Adrienne followed his gaze. Sure enough, a knobby-tired purple mountain bike lay on its side across two beams.

"Perfect," Adrienne said. Then she glanced down at her skirt. "Except that I couldn't ride in this."

"I'll fetch the bike down while you git a pair of Dorothy's jeans and one of her more ordinary tops," Archie said.

Adrienne hesitated. "Are you sure, Archie? I can tell how much you cared about Dorothy, and I feel bad rummaging through her things like this."

Archie glanced away. "You're a lot like her. Seems fittin' fer you to wear them clothes. Now git on in there, so you kin find Matt afore he gits himself kilt."

His reminder of Matt's being in danger was all it took to send Adrienne dashing back to the house. She'd finished dressing in jeans and a blue western blouse with lace trim when Archie rapped on the door.

"You 'bout ready?" he called. "I made you some peanut butter sandwiches. You kin take 'em with."

"Sounds great," she called back, and crossed to open the door.

He gazed at her for a moment. "You shore do put me in mind of Dorothy," he said, handing her a sack that smelled of peanut butter. "I 'specially see it when you and Matt go at each other. Dorothy and me usta fight like that, but we . . . well, it ain't important."

"You were about to say you loved each other," Adrienne prompted.

"I guess so." Archie didn't look at her.

"It's nothing to be embarrassed about, Archie. I think it's wonderful how much you cared, how much you still care for her."

Archie's chest heaved. "You oughta grab that Matt fella, and you two oughta never let go. Life's short."

"I'm beginning to believe you're right."

"Dorothy and me, we spent too much time fightin', too, same as you and Matt. Me complainin' that she read too many books, her sayin' I had none a that—what you call it?—culture." He looked at her, his eyes moist. "Why couldn't we like each other the way we was?"

"I guess that's human nature, to try to change people," Adrienne said. "I'm sure she knew that you loved her, Archie. And she loved you, in spite of her complaining about your lack of culture."

"But she was right! I ain't got no culture. My favorite food's peanut butter. I chaw tobacco an' I drink whiskey. Lots of whiskey. Besides, see that ugly clock?" He gestured behind him into the living room where the plastic grapes, cheese, and wine bottle hung on the wall. "That thing was my weddin' present to her. I thought it was beautiful. 'Fore long I knowed what she thought of it. She hated it."

"Then why didn't she take it down, if she hated it so much?"

"Dang if I know. I told her to enough times."

"Then why don't you take it down now?"

"Dunno." Archie looked away. "Don't seem right."

"Because it was your wedding present to her. I think she loved it, Archie, just because you gave it to her."

"Naw. She hated it."

Adrienne gazed at the clock. Twenty to four. She had to hurry. "I'd better be going, Archie," she said, keeping her tone gentle. She didn't want him to think she was brushing him off, just as he was confiding his feelings about his dead wife, but Matt's life could be in danger.

"Shore. Git goin'." He stood without moving and stared at the floor. He seemed lost in his memories of Dorothy.

Adrienne eased past him and walked through the living room. She reached for the doorknob.

"Wait," Archie said. "I got somethin' else to tell you."

Adrienne turned, trying not to show her impatience.

"You bein' a woman and all, and you're like Dorothy, so you might be able to figure this out. Wait there." He went back into the bedroom.

A glance at the clock made her increasingly nervous. Still, she owed Archie the courtesy of waiting.

He returned with a slip of paper, which he held out to her. "You make anythin' of this?"

She glanced at the handwritten message, a woman's handwriting, she thought.

A cygnet is homely to all but its mother. She needs not the swan's grace; it's but a fine cover to what has been there since the very beginning, a heart that is true, a way that is winning.

"It's a poem, I guess," Adrienne said.

"It's a riddle. Dorothy's riddle."

"For what?" Adrienne studied the poem again.

Archie shuffled his feet. "Me and Dorothy had a fight. Don't even know what about, now, but she was boilin' mad. Took all my gold and hid it."

Adrienne's head snapped up. Jeb and Curtis had been babbling something about gold, but she hadn't paid any attention.

"This here riddle is s'posed to be a clue," Archie said, "but I can't figure the danged thing out. Don't much feel like it, neither, t'tell the truth."

"And Dorothy never told you the answer?"

"She woulda, sooner or later, 'cept for the heart attack. One minit she was here, the next minit she weren't. Died mad, too. That's what gits me."

Adrienne put her hand on his arm. "I'm sorry, Archie."

"Yep." He sighed. "What's done is done. Think you kin figure out the clue?"

"I can try." Adrienne read it through again, committing the words to memory.

"I never showed it to nobody before. Didn't trust 'em. But you and Matt, you're like Dorothy and me."

"I won't tell anyone," Adrienne said.

"I know you won't. That's why I showed you the riddle. You kin tell Matt, though. If'n you two figure it out, you kin have half."

Adrienne stared at him. "Half the gold?"

"Yep. Half. Don't have no need fer it, anyways."

"We couldn't do that, Archie. It's your gold."

"Better not speak out of turn. Ain't Matt's plane at the bottom of the canyon?"

Adrienne realized Archie was offering Matt a chance to recoup his losses. She shouldn't speak for Matt, and if anyone deserved half of Archie's gold, Matt did. "I'd better get out there," she said. "I'll think about the riddle on the way."

"Jist foller the tire tracks," Archie said. "You'll find him. The bike has them thorn-proof tires, so you shouldn't have no blowouts."

"Thanks, Archie." Adrienne squeezed his arm. "You've been wonderful."

"Dorothy woulda wanted it that way."

"Dorothy was pretty wonderful, too, wasn't she?" Adrienne wondered if he'd revert to calling his late wife "ornery."

"Yep," Archie said, "pretty danged wonderful," and he turned away.

Adrienne could tell Archie's emotions were getting the best of him, and he didn't like it. "Matt and I will be back soon," she said, and left the cabin.

Archie had polished the dust from the purple mountain bike and leaned it against the porch. It had a small carrier on the back, and Adrienne strapped the bag of sandwiches on it before grasping the handlebars and climbing on. Although she hadn't ridden a bicycle in years, the technique came back quickly. She pedaled out through the break in the fence.

In daylight, and on relatively dry road, she made fast progress to the point where Matt had turned off into the desert. After that she dodged around rocks, bushes, and an occasional prickly pear cactus, but Matt's tire tracks made finding a path fairly easy.

She couldn't believe the difference between their miserable trek the night before, and now, dressed in appropriate clothes and riding a bike through late-afternoon sunshine. Even the sandy wash, once filled with a raging torrent that had prompted Matt to sling her over his shoulder, had slowed to a trickle that she crossed at a spot where several rocks formed a natural bridge.

As the shadowed canyon drew near, she saw Archie's truck parked near the edge of the mesa and recognized the gnarled juniper tree that marked the spot where the plane had nose-dived into oblivion. Matt was nowhere around. She realized that in order to find him she might have to go right up to the edge of the chasm. Her stomach knotted. She hadn't thought this mission through to its possible conclusion; neither had she taken her acrophobia into account. Concern for Matt's welfare had driven out all caution . . . again.

Telling herself that she and Matt wouldn't behave this way once they returned to civilization, Adrienne leaned the bike against the truck and unstrapped the sandwiches. Then she carefully approached the gnarled tree. "Matt?" she called.

No answer. A rope was knotted around the tree trunk and hung over the edge of the mesa.

"Matt, are you down there?" she called again.

Only the moan of the wind in the canyon answered her. A hawk circled overhead. She studied it and decided it wasn't a hawk at all, but a buzzard. She shivered.

Finally she accepted the idea that she'd have to go over to the tree and pull up on the rope. Matt might be dangling at the other end, and the wind might have prevented him from hearing her. She walked part of the way, but then got down on her knees, put the sandwich bag between her teeth and crawled the last few feet.

She didn't look out, but only down at the rock-strewn ground under her hands and feet. By lifting her gaze a little, she could see the tree, its exposed roots clutching the edge of the mesa like a witch's fingers.

By the time she reached the tree she was on her stomach. Dust filled her nostrils and she prayed she wouldn't come face-to-face with a snake. Closing her eyes, she fumbled for the rope and pulled. The rope offered no resistance. Placing the sandwich bag carefully beside her, she called his name again and lay very still, waiting for an answer.

Nothing. The canyon seemed to have swallowed him as it had the plane. She tried not to think of him lying at the bottom of the canyon, his body twisted by the impact, his bones crushed—oh, God, she had to find him. He might be alive and needing her help. She had to get to him. She wouldn't be able to lift him out, but she could apply a tourniquet or a splint and go for help. She'd take the sandwiches, in case he needed nourishment.

Wiggling closer to the tree, she embraced its alligator-hide trunk. From here she'd have a view over the edge. She wouldn't allow herself to think what would happen if the tree came loose. After all, it had been clinging there for years. Surely it could hold on a little longer and keep her from tumbling over the edge.

She held her breath and peered around a clump of dry grass blocking her view.

9

ADRIENNE EXPECTED a steep drop to the wrecked plane which, if she could see it at all, would be lying like a broken toy at the bottom of the canyon. Instead she was staring at a ledge about three stories below her where the plane sat right side up. Except for one wing that had been torn off and lay beside the fuselage, and a tail section that seemed a little ragged, the plane appeared to be in good shape.

Apparently it had flipped over once before landing on the widest section of the ledge, nose pointing out toward the canyon. If a salvage crew with helicopters could lift the plane and its damaged wing off the ledge, Matt could have it repaired. Adrienne couldn't believe his luck. But where was he?

She called his name again and received no answer. The plane took up most of the ledge, leaving very little room for walking around and almost nowhere that he could be hidden from view. Besides, he should have heard her by now. As she called into the canyon, her voice echoed. Someone would have to be deaf not to hear. Deaf or...

She refused to complete the thought. Instead she looked at the rope dangling down to the ledge. Somehow she had to climb down it. It was the only way she could find out what had happened to Matt.

Slowly she rose to her knees and picked up the sandwiches. Opening the top two buttons of her shirt, she shoved the sack inside. The sandwiches might get squashed, but they'd be better than nothing in an emergency.

Concentrating on Matt, she stood and grasped the rope. In high school she'd shimmied up and down ropes in gym class, hating every minute of the exercise. But in gym class the ropes had been thicker, and mats had been spread underneath, in case anyone should fall. Adrienne decided to pretend she had thick, protective mats below her on the ledge.

She'd also seen film clips of people rappelling down cliffs, and she remembered that to begin they held the rope taut and backed over the edge. That would be good. She didn't want to see what was happening beneath her.

Fluffy, thick mats lie below me, she repeated silently to herself. She leaned back against the rope and fumbled with her moccasined foot for a toehold below the ledge. Her heartbeat drummed in her ears. She found the first spot, and then a second. Her fingers began to ache, and she'd barely started down.

A little more. Then more. Her face was even with the edge, then below it. All she could see were chunks of striated rock, brick-reds laced with flinty gray, and patches of rust-colored dirt. Moisture gathered on her upper lip. Fear left a metallic taste in her mouth.

Down she went, inch by painful inch, gripping the rope with fingers growing numb. Her arms ached; the sockets pulled painfully, and she remembered a doll she'd once had whose arms had popped right off its body.

A beige horny toad the size of a half-dollar skittered past her nose and she cried out, more startled than scared. But the distraction made her lose her footing and she banged against the rocks, scraping her cheek. Gasping with fear, she scrambled for a toehold and lost a moccasin. It landed on the ledge below with a soft, hollow plop, reminding her of the space between her body and the ledge. A breeze from the canyon chilled her sweat-dampened body.

Fluffy, thick mats lie below me, she thought again, but she no longer believed it. A rocky ledge lay beneath her, and a narrow one at that. If the fall didn't kill her, she might roll just a little and tumble over the lip.

She froze in place, unwilling to move her hands, but at last the pain in her arms drove her to unclench her fingers and start downward once more. She should have ridden the bicycle back for help instead of tackling this on her own. Once down, if she made it, she'd never be able to climb the rope back to the top. Matt might need help, but hers wasn't worth much.

Her palms burned from the friction of the coarse rope and her legs shook, but the distance to the top grew longer. At last she chanced a look down, and noticed the ledge was less than ten feet away. Still she couldn't risk letting go and dropping that far. The landing space wasn't wide enough to ensure she wouldn't fall off the edge.

"Matt!" she called, moving her hands more rapidly down the rope. "Matt, I'm here!"

When he didn't answer, her stomach churned with fear. Only one thing could explain his silence. But she couldn't lose him now. Life wouldn't be so cruel as to take him away just when she'd realized how precious he was to her. She'd find him, wherever he was. She'd rescue him, as long as he wasn't... But of course he was alive. She wouldn't believe otherwise.

Her bare foot touched solid ground. She was down. Releasing the rope, she sat down hard, not even minding the sharp rock that bit into her thigh. Her palms were red, and the one she'd scraped the night before was bleeding again. She stared at the blood as her whole body began to shake. "I did it," she whispered, and lifted her gaze all the way to the top. Reaction gradually gave way to triumph. "I did it!" she shouted, and stood up on unsteady legs to locate Dorothy's other moccasin.

Once she had both feet protected again, she turned toward the plane. There, in the cockpit, was Matt, headset covering his ears as he fiddled with the dials of the radio. He'd changed into a rust-colored shirt, but it was Matt all right. She'd know that dark curly hair and chiseled profile anywhere.

Her throat constricted and relief brought tears to her eyes. He was alive. He was fine. He hadn't heard her because that damned headset had been covering his ears.

Of course, if he'd taken it off once or twice, he would have heard her calling to him. She wouldn't have had to climb down the rope. Adrienne gazed at her stinging, bleeding hands and looked back at the plane. She'd risked her life for nothing. Matt didn't need her at all.

Striding over to the plane, she opened the pilot's door and tugged on his sleeve.

When he saw her, Matt nearly leaped out of his seat. "Where in hell did you come from?" he yelled, pulling off the headset.

She pointed back toward the rope.

"Why?"

"Because I was worried about you, you stupid idiot! I came to the edge and called and called, but of course you didn't answer, because you had that thing on," she pointed to it as if it were a malodorous skunk. "So what else could I do?"

He stared at her. "What else indeed? What's that sticking out of your shirt?"

"Peanut butter sandwiches!" she yelled, yanking them out and flinging them at him.

He caught the sandwich bag as if it were a football. "Of course," he said, sounding dazed. "Burnham, I don't believe this. You're petrified of heights and I'll bet you've never rappelled down a cliff in your life."

"Which is why I should have pedaled Dorothy's bike right back to the house and found help there."

"You rode a bike out here?" Matt tossed the sandwiches on the seat and climbed down from the cockpit.

"Yes, fool that I am. Although at least I have some experience riding a bike. But coming down that rope was the dumbest, most unnecessary thing I've ever done in my life, and I wrecked my hands, and—"

"And your cheek," Matt said, tucking his finger under her chin and tilting her head toward the light. "You scraped your cheek."

"I lost my footing once." His touch unnerved her, but she didn't want him to know, so she kept babbling. "It's a miracle I didn't fall into the canyon, as little as I know about all this."

He stared at her. "Just exactly how did you climb down the rope?"

"I just held on and moved my hands down. How else would I do it?"

"You didn't tie the rope around your waist before you started down?"

"No. Was I supposed to?"

He groaned and wrapped his arms around her. "Good God, woman," he murmured, tucking her head against his chest.

She began to tremble, both from reaction and the excitement of being back in his arms. "Next time I'd appreciate it if you wouldn't shut out the world when you get yourself into some dangerous situation, like out on this ledge," she said, her words muffled against his shirt. "Next time—"

"Do you think there will be a next time, Adrienne?" he asked, laying his cheek against her hair. "Do you plan to make a habit of saving me?"

Her heartbeat accelerated. "I sure hope not. I hope you won't need my help again. It is getting ridiculous."

"That's for sure. But you know, Adrienne, I wonder why you'd risk your life for some guy who wasn't particularly suitable for you."

She hesitated, wondering if he'd forgive her. "I should never have said those things," she said at last.

"Oh?"

"I . . . I had no right to pass judgment like that, especially after all you'd done to help me. And besides, I think I might have been wrong about a few things."

His chest heaved as he took a deep breath. "Maybe a few." He leaned down and placed a gentle kiss beside the scrape on her cheek. "But it doesn't matter now. You came to find me today. You foolish, crazy woman." He tipped her face up and his lips moved like a whisper of feathers across her cheek.

"I couldn't let you come out here alone."

"That's good to know." He nibbled the corner of her mouth.

"I was afraid . . . that something bad might have happened to you."

He outlined her mouth with the tip of his tongue. "Nothing bad has happened to me, but if you can stop talking for a minute, something good might."

"Oh, Matt," she sighed. "I'm so very glad you're alive."

"Me, too," he said, and settled his mouth over hers.

She fit against him with remembered perfection, and when he kissed her, she knew he'd forgiven her for the terrible things she'd said to him. The possessive thrust of his tongue told her that he still wanted her as he had the night before in the barn. Joyfully she responded, pressing herself against the lean strength of his body. His hands roved over her, caressing her hips and her bottom before sliding up to cup her breasts.

He lifted his head and gazed down at her. "You really have changed your mind about me."

"Yes." Her breath caught in her throat at the look in his hazel eyes.

"Adrienne, it can be so good between us."

She held his gaze. "I know that now."

"I want you. Right here. Right this minute." He rubbed his thumbs over her nipples. "And we have nothing. No cozy barn, no blanket, no straw, nothing."

"And maybe snakes," she said.

"Snakes?" He grew still. "I hadn't thought of that."

She chuckled. "You'd be bothered by a few snakes? Fearless Matt Kirkland?"

"Let's just say I don't relish taking off the number of clothes that would be required for what I have in mind if we have to worry about snakebite."

Adrienne nestled closer. "We won't be down here forever."

"That's for sure. In fact, I think we should start back up right now. The radio's not working at all. We'll get our wallets out of the plane and head up to the top."

"I—I'm not sure I can make it. My hands . . ."

"I'll pull you up. I'll go first and drop a sling down for you." He took one of her hands in his and studied the palm. "We can't have any more of this rough stuff happening to you."

"Although I've learned a lot, and I'm much braver than I was."

He smiled down at her. "No, not braver. You've always been that. You're the bravest woman I know."

"Matt, I—"

"Shh." He laid his finger over her lips. "Did you hear that?"

"What?" She looked around wildly. No one could be on this narrow ledge with them.

"Up on top. A truck."

She strained her ears and caught the faint sound of an engine. The sound grew louder and stopped. Doors slammed, the echo reverberating to them. She glanced at Matt. He was frowning.

"Hey, city boy!"

"Great," Matt said, keeping his voice low. "Jeb and Curtis have found us. Back up against the face of the canyon. Maybe they won't see you."

She stared at him, her eyes wide. "Surely they wouldn't come down here?" she whispered.

"Curtis might, with you as the reason."

Adrienne shuddered.

"But probably not," he added, glancing at her with sympathy. "He's too fat and out of shape."

"They'll be mad, though, after you sent them on a wild-goose chase."

"Undoubtedly. I'd planned to be through and out of here before they caught on, but I overslept." He winked at her. "The barn was real comfortable."

She made a face and he chuckled.

"Hey, you down there!"

Matt backed away from Adrienne and glanced up, shading his eyes. "What do you want, Jeb?"

"Better directions, for starters," Jeb called back.

"Sorry about that."

"Yeah, I'll jist bet you are. Say what's Dorothy's mountain bike doin' out here?"

Adrienne flattened herself against the face of the canyon.

"I brought it in the back of the truck," Matt said, "just for good measure. Didn't know if the truck would make it through the underbrush all the way to the edge of the mesa. Turns out it did."

"I think you're lyin'. I think you got that little gal down there with ya," Jeb said.

"Are you kidding? A woman like her? If you think I'm a wimp, you should see her. She's afraid of heights. She wouldn't shimmy down that rope if her life depended on it."

Adrienne held her breath.

"Yeah, guess you're right," Jeb said. "Curtis seemed t'think she might foller you down there, but I say she wouldn't. Them city gals ain't got no trainin' in that sort of thing."

"That's right," Matt called back, and grinned at Adrienne. "They're not good for much."

She glared at him and his smile grew broader.

"They's good for jist one thing," Jeb said. "And that one thing is what ol' Curtis wants. Where is she, anyways?"

"Hightailing it back to Tucson, where she belongs," Matt said. "Called somebody to come and pick her up as soon as the phone lines dried."

"Figures," Jeb said. "Well, see'n as how you're down there all alone, guess we'll leave you that way. Oh, 'cept for one thing."

Adrienne saw Matt's expression change from laughter to rage.

"You sonofabitch! Leave that alone!" he shouted, rushing toward the rope.

"Maybe next time you won't jack around with ol' Jeb and ol' Curtis," came the reply, and the cut rope cascaded at Matt's feet.

Adrienne stared at the tangled rope. They had no way out.

As the sound of the truck's motor faded away, she noted that the sun had almost disappeared beyond the opposite wall of the canyon. Slowly she walked over to Matt, who was still staring at the rope, which was lying at his feet like a large and very uncoordinated earthworm. "Well, what now?" she asked.

He glanced at her. "Bad choice of words. The last time you said that, it started to rain."

Adrienne looked up. "Not much chance of that, but dusk is when the snakes come out."

"Maybe we should sit in the plane."

"Is it safe? Could it . . . tip over again?"

He gazed at her. "You know, I hadn't even thought of that. You have such a talent for predicting disaster."

"You mean you sat in the cockpit for Lord knows how long, fiddling with the radio, and never considered that a sudden gust of wind might blow you over the edge?"

"Yes, I guess that's what I did."

"I don't think I want to sit in the plane," Adrienne said, eyeing it suspiciously.

"Well, I, for one, don't want to spend the night out here with the snakes."

"The night? We won't be here all night. Archie will come out to get us when we don't show up."

Matt hooked his thumbs in his belt loops and looked at her. "How? We have his truck. And you have his wife's mountain bike. How's he going to get here? Unless that burro he's having delivered—"

"No," Adrienne said, shaking her head. "He told me before I left that the burro wasn't broken to ride yet. You're right. Archie can't come to get us."

"Shall we sit in the plane, then?"

Adrienne studied the plane's position. The landing gear looked far too close to the edge for her comfort. She shook her head. "Not me. I wish you wouldn't, either."

Matt glanced at the plane and back at Adrienne. "Okay," he said with a sigh.

Adrienne's stomach picked that moment to grumble.

"Are you hungry?" he asked, smiling at her.

"I guess I am. Come to think of it, I haven't had any food since Beverly's party."

"Boy, does that seem centuries ago. Well, you're in luck. We happen to have peanut butter sandwiches and a canteen of water Archie insisted I bring along. I'll get them out of the plane and we can sit down over there, with our backs to the cliff. Then we can see the snakes coming while we eat," he said wryly.

"It's late in the year," she called after him as he went to retrieve their dinner. "Maybe the snakes are all hibernating." She was touched that he'd sit out here with her instead of climbing in the plane where he felt safer.

"Let's hope," he said, returning with the sandwich bag and a metal canteen on a strap.

They found a smooth stretch of dirt and leaned against the still-warm rocks.

"Here you go," he said, handing her a wad of bread and peanut butter. "One mangled sandwich."

"Don't insult the sandwiches that I risked my life to bring down here," she said, taking a large bite that tasted wonderful.

"Don't remind me." He smiled as he watched her eat. "In fact, considering where those sandwiches were stashed during the trip, I'd say they're pure gold."

"Gold!" She glanced up at him, her mouth partly full. "I almost forgot about Archie's gold!"

"Say that again?"

"Remember when Curtis and Jeb were accusing us of being after Archie's gold? There really is some, except that Dorothy hid it while they were having a fight, and then she died before she could tell him where she'd put it."

"You're kidding."

"Honest to God. Archie told me."

"You're sure he wasn't into the sauce when he told you that?"

"He looked perfectly sober to me, Matt. And besides that, he said if we helped him find the gold, he'd give us half."

"Now I really don't believe it. Why would he do that?"

"Because he—" She saw something move behind him. "Be still," she cautioned. "Just stay still."

His voice sounded as if he didn't have quite enough air. "It's a snake, isn't it? I know it's a snake."

"Yes, but I think he'll go right on by if we don't move."

"He?" The question squeaked at the end. "How the hell can you tell if it's a boy snake or a girl snake?"

"I can't. It was a figure of speech."

"How close?"

"About six feet behind you. No, don't turn around."

Sweat beaded Matt's forehead. "Tell me it's one of those harmless gopher snakes."

Although dusk was swiftly falling in the canyon, Adrienne could make out the triangular-shaped head of the approaching snake. Its patterned tan-and-brown length of four or five feet ended with a striped section of tail and several rattles. "It's not a gopher snake," she said.

"Just my luck." Matt licked his lips. "Is it looking at me?"

"No. His tongue's flicking out, so he's sensing your heat, though."

"Wonderful. How can you stay so calm? One bite from that snake, with no place to go for help, and one of us could die out here."

"He won't bite us if we're careful. He's passing through. Don't make any sudden moves and he won't feel threatened."

"I'm so glad. What about how threatened I feel?"

The snake changed course and slithered over toward the Cessna. "There," Adrienne said. "Now you can look. He's over by the landing gear."

Matt slowly turned his head and gasped. "A monster! What kind is it?"

"It's a rattlesnake. I take it you've never met one in the wild."

"I take it you've met hundreds. I feel like I'm on a segment of *Wild Kingdom*."

"When you ride horseback you usually come across snakes. They aren't always rattlesnakes, but some are.

I've learned if I leave them alone, they'll leave me alone. See? There he goes," she said as the snake glided along the ledge and slipped through a crevice at the end.

Matt let out his breath. "Sure you wouldn't like to sit in the plane?"

"I'd rather take my chances out here. Now be honest. Was that so frightening?"

"Yes."

Adrienne smiled at him. "I never thought I'd see the day when your cockiness disappeared."

"I never thought I'd see the day when you'd loosen up enough to let me love you," he countered, gazing at her.

She looked into his eyes and couldn't look away again. Desire pulsed between them, an energetic force demanding to be obeyed.

He rose to his knees and pulled her with him. "This is impossible," he said, wrapping his arms around her. "We may be here all night, and I'm kidding myself if I think I can make it through without holding you and kissing the daylights out of you. I can't go all night without making love to you."

"What about the snakes?" she whispered.

His smile was crooked. "Damn the snakes, Burnham," he said, cupping her bottom and pressing her against the fullness of his groin. "Full speed ahead."

10

THE MOIST temptation of Adrienne's peanut butter-flavored kiss drove out all Matt's worries about snakes. He closed his eyes and gave himself up to the sensation of her soft lips parting, her arms tightening, her body molding to his. Her willing surrender excited him, but his feelings ran deeper than excitement. She valued him so much that today she'd risked her life to rescue him from imagined dangers. The evidence that she cared was a more powerful aphrodisiac than any other. He ached for her.

His fingers trembled, and his attempt to unfasten the buttons of her blouse met with only partial success. Her slender hand closed over his fumbling. "Let me," she whispered against his mouth. Leaning away, she kept her gaze on his as she undid the buttons. After discarding the blouse, she slowly drew the camisole over her head and tossed it aside, too.

He almost forgot to breathe. The first time, in the barn, he'd been too frenzied to really look at her. Touch had given him tactile knowledge, but now, seeing the proud thrust of her breasts bathed in the rose light of sunset, he vowed never to be so hasty again. Her gaze invited his caress, but he held off for a moment more. "You're magnificent," he said.

She reached for his hands and cupped them under her breasts. "I want you to love me," she murmured.

"I know. That makes all the difference."

She looked into his eyes, and her lips parted. He waited, wondering if she would say aloud what he read in her gaze. But she wasn't ready to say it. Instead she closed her eyes and threw back her head as he gently supported her breasts and brushed his thumbs over her nipples. Gradually they tightened into hard buds of desire.

He leaned down to taste her, first exploring with his tongue as her breath came faster. Then slowly he drew one nipple into his mouth and moaned at the sweetness of her warm, scented skin. She tangled her fingers in his hair and urged him closer. Hollowing his cheeks he took more of her and felt the rapid pace of her heartbeat under the press of his hand.

He supported her with his arm and she arched backward in a gesture of surrender that made his loins burn. He was ravenous, sucking and nipping at her breasts that grew pink from the friction of his loving. He aroused her until she was gasping and need pushed at him more fiercely than he ever remembered before.

"Please," she whispered.

He reached for the metal button of her jeans. Then he paused. Not here, not on the ground. Perhaps with her back to the canyon wall. A smooth stretch of rock. He nearly went crazy imagining himself thrusting forward, burying himself in her softness, exulting in her love. For that was what she was offering him. That was the emotion driving them to this wild coupling.

He lifted her by her elbows as he staggered upright. "Over there," he murmured, urging her backward. In the dim light he found the spot he wanted, a sun-warmed stretch of smooth brown stone that wouldn't abrade her tender skin. Such tender skin. Kissing her mouth, her eyes, her throat, he eased her back with his arm braced behind her. With his other hand he snapped open her jeans and drew the zipper down.

He eased his hand beneath her panties and discovered the welcome moisture that signaled how much she wanted him. He kissed her hard and thoroughly while he built her desire to a fever pitch with rhythmic caresses. He and Adrienne seemed at one with the night sounds—the crickets pulsed in time to his stroking fingers; the rustle of bat wings echoed her breathless gasps; the braying of a burro...Matt paused and lifted his head to listen. The braying of a burro?

"What was that noise?" Adrienne asked.

"Nothing," Matt said, deciding he'd imagined it, deciding he couldn't go another second without the ecstasy of sinking into her. "Adrienne, I need you. We need each other." He wrenched open the fastener of his jeans. The sound came again.

"Matt, that was a braying noise. Like a burro."

"Probably Yosemite Sam," Matt said, struggling with his zipper one-handed. "Adrienne—"

"Matt, somebody's singing."

With superhuman effort Matt stopped to listen. Braying and singing filled the silence. Sighing, Matt gave up the fight and leaned his forehead against Adrienne's. "Seems to me I've heard that tune before."

"Under slightly different circumstances."

Matt's chest heaved. "You might say that."

"He's come to fetch us home, Matt," Adrienne said. Then after a moment she began to laugh.

Matt didn't feel like laughing. "His heart's in the right place, but his timing stinks."

"Oh, Matt, I'm sorry."

"That makes two of us."

"Maybe . . . maybe we'd better put our clothes back on," she said gently, disengaging his hand from beneath her panties.

Turning, Matt sagged against the rock face next to Adrienne. Archie had just slammed the door to paradise in his face. The burro brayed again. "Will you listen to that animal?" Matt said, fastening his jeans with difficulty. "Dorothy the third is not happy about this trip."

The burro's protests sounded like someone trying to get water from a rusty hand pump, and Adrienne laughed harder.

Matt glanced sideways at her. "I like the way your breasts move when you laugh," he said. "Very soon we'll get back to this. When that happens, remind me to make you laugh."

"How will I be able to help it? All I have to do is think of all we've been through in the past twenty-four hours and I'll be rolling on the floor."

"That sounds like fun, too," Matt said, gazing at her.

"Everything sounds like fun, doesn't it?" she asked softly.

"More than fun. I wish. . . ." Matt glanced up as the volume of Archie's singing increased.

"We'd better get dressed."

"Right." Reluctantly he leaned down and retrieved her camisole. "Here's your silky little number."

Adrienne pulled it over her head. "You know, I never told you the rest of the story about the gold."

"Who wants to hear boring old stories about gold when I can be enjoying other things? Besides, I don't believe there is any gold."

"I do." Adrienne picked up her blouse and shook it out. "Archie showed me a riddle Dorothy had written to give him a clue to where she'd hidden it."

"Oh, yeah?"

"It said—let me see—

A cygnet is homely to all but its mother. She needs not the swan's grace; it's but a fine cover to what has been loved since the very beginning, a heart that is true, a way that is winning.

"A cygnet's a baby swan, right?"

"Right."

"So this is a riddle about swans? I didn't notice any chickens around Archie's place, let alone swans."

"I know. I'm not sure what it means, either, except that I know Archie wants to solve that riddle, and not just for the gold."

Matt chuckled. "Because he doesn't want Dorothy to have the last word?"

"Maybe that, too, but this riddle is a sort of communication from the grave. He wants to know what she meant."

"Now you've got me curious."

"Good, maybe on the ride back we can—"

"Hello down below!" Archie called, shining the kerosene lantern over the edge. Then he guffawed loudly. "I made me a rhyme. *Hello down below.* How 'bout that? Rhymin' deserves another snort, don'tcha think?"

"Great, he's drunk," Matt said in a low voice. "Hey, Archie," he called, "don't get too near the drop-off. Move on back from the edge."

"That you, Matt?" Archie's face appeared at the rim of the canyon, lit by the kerosene lamp. He appeared to be lying down.

"It's me. And Adrienne. Now move on back, Archie, before you end up down here with us."

"Ain't gonna fall." The burro brayed some more. "Shut up, Dorothy," Archie demanded. "You hear that, Matt? She's jist like my ornery wife, always somethin' t'say. Throwed me off three times on the way out here. Luckily I'd had a few snorts so it didn't hurt much."

Adrienne gazed up at Archie's face peering over the edge. "I thought Dorothy wasn't broken to ride yet?"

"She ain't, but I informed her she had t'git me out here. You two was late. Speakin' of which, Matt, it's gittin' mighty dark. Why don'tcha come up now?"

"Jeb and Curtis cut our rope. We're stuck."

"Oh. Them skunks. Shoulda knowed. Hey, want me t'lower down this here whiskey bottle? Bet you could use a snort, too."

"You have a rope?" Matt called.

"Shore. I'll jist tie it t'the neck of this bottle, and then—"

"Wait. We don't need the bottle, just the rope. Can you tie it to the tree and let it down?"

"Shore."

Adrienne touched Matt's sleeve. "What if he doesn't tie it tight? If he's sloshed, he might not do such a good job."

"We have to take that chance. Archie's in danger out here, too. It's a wonder he made it on that crotchety burro, and I wouldn't give much for his chances going back. We both know about the snakes, not to mention the possibility of his hitting his head on a rock the next time Dorothy tosses him off."

Adrienne sighed. "I suppose you're right, but I don't like it."

"I'll go first." He walked over to the Cessna. "When we pull you up, you can carry my wallet." He reached in and retrieved their things from the back seat of the plane. "Here. Just stick my wallet in your purse."

"Matt, I don't like your going up that rope. I don't want anything to happen to Archie, either, but more than that I don't want anything to happen to you."

He grabbed her quickly and kissed her. "It won't," he said. "I have a few important things left to do in this life, one of which is finally, without interruption, to make love to you the whole blessed night."

"Here comes the rope!" Archie called.

Matt walked over to the cliff face and gave the rope a tug. "Did you tie it tight, Archie?"

"Shore."

Matt knotted the rope around his waist. "This is what you were supposed to do before you came down the first time," he said, glancing at Adrienne. "I still can't believe you shimmied down with nothing to keep you from falling."

"Pretty stupid."

"Pretty courageous. Now, when I get back up, I'll retie this end into a sling with a loop for each leg. Put it on and we'll pull you up so you don't have to work so hard this time."

Adrienne looked up to the top of the cliff where the kerosene lantern illuminated the gnarled branches of the juniper and Archie crouched beside it. "I hate this, Matt."

He tested the rope one more time. "Like I said, I have tremendous motivation to succeed. Now, stand back."

"Why do I have to stand back if you're not going to fall?"

He gazed at her. "You ask too many questions, Burnham. Just stand back, okay?"

ADRIENNE MOVED AWAY, her heart pounding. Matt didn't know if the rope would hold him or not, but he was going up anyway.

She held her breath and watched as he grasped the rope and positioned one booted foot three feet up on the cliff face. Then he lifted himself off the ground and started up the rope, hand over hand, his feet scrabbling for purchase against the rock. Soon he was a dark shadow growing smaller and less distinct. Adrienne's breath came in shallow gasps as she stood rigidly with clenched hands and willed him to the top.

I love him, she thought, straining to retain her sight of him in the shadows. *I love that man. Please let him be safe*. When she saw his head silhouetted in the light from Archie's lantern as he grasped the root of a tree to haul himself over the edge, tears trickled down her cheeks. "Thank you," she whispered. "Thank you."

"Adrienne?" he called, turning back to gaze down into the canyon. "You ready?"

"I sure am," she said, her voice choked with emotion. "For anything."

She heard his deep chuckle echo through the canyon. How she loved him.

Her trip up the side of the canyon was much easier than her trip down had been, but still her stomach muscles tensed at the thought of hanging over thin air. Matt had tied the rope to the axle of the truck and had Archie drive slowly away from the cliff, but he had braced himself and kept a good hold on the rope in case Archie's feet slipped on the pedals.

When Adrienne reached the top, Matt hauled her into his arms and held her tight.

"I thought you said you weren't worried?" she murmured, her cheek pressed against his shirt where she could hear his heart hammering in his chest.

"You think I would tell you how worried I was?" he asked, kissing her hair.

"So you were."

"I was terrified."

"Now you tell me."

"Now I'll tell you all sorts of things," he said. "Adrienne, I—"

"Shore was a neat trick," Archie said, swaggering over to them and spitting tobacco juice in the dirt. "Want a nip, now?"

"No, thanks," Matt said. "I think we'd better—" He paused. "Archie, did you put on the emergency brake?"

"Why?"

"The truck's rolling backward!" Matt yelled, and raced for the cab.

Adrienne couldn't move. With agonizing clarity she saw what would happen if Matt didn't stop the truck. He would go over the edge with it, and she, still attached to the rope tied to the axle, would be pulled down, too.

The truck rolled toward the cliff. Adrienne watched in fascinated horror as Matt clambered into the cab. Then, with a shudder, the truck stopped. Matt climbed down slowly and walked over to her as if in a trance.

"Thanks. If you hadn't stopped the truck, this rope would have taken me over the edge."

"You might want to take the rope off," he said, his face white.

"Good idea." She fumbled with the knot but her fingers were shaking. Finally the knots loosened and she stepped out of the sling Matt had created to keep her safe.

"Close call," Archie said, looking rattled, too. "Sorry 'bout that."

Matt sighed and ran his fingers through his hair. "Let's load Dorothy and the bike in back of the truck and go home."

"Dorothy won't like it none."

"Then we'll tie her behind and go slow," Matt said. He glanced at Archie. "And I'll drive."

Archie returned his stare. "Shore," he said, and nodded.

At Matt's insistence, Adrienne sat in the cab while Archie and Matt tied Dorothy, braying constantly, to the back bumper. After they loaded the mountain bike,

Matt climbed into the driver's seat and Archie sat on the other side of Adrienne. Archie smelled as much like a brewery as he had the night before, and he kept rolling down the window to spit, but Adrienne found she didn't mind so much this time.

"Shore am sorry 'bout that brake," Archie said again as they started off.

"It's okay," Adrienne said, patting his arm. "Accidents happen."

"I coulda never faced Dorothy if'n you'd—well, anyways."

"We're all here, safe and sound," Matt said. From behind them, the burro brayed loudly. "Even Dorothy the third."

Adrienne put a hand on Matt's knee. She had to touch him and reassure herself he was there beside her. Matt reached down and guided her hand higher on his thigh, and she flushed but kept her hand where he wanted it.

"What's that about a riddle with swans in it, Archie?" Matt asked.

"I ain't been able to figure it out," Archie said, sounding forlorn. "We ain't got no swans. This here's the desert."

"Pictures of swans?" Adrienne asked.

Archie shook his head. "Not even in her books. I looked. 'Course she couldn't hide no gold in them books, 'cept by cuttin' out pages. She wouldn't do that. Dorothy loved them books."

"How many pages would she have to cut out, Archie?" Matt asked.

"'Bout all of 'em from one of her big ol' books."

Matt whistled. "That's a lot of gold."

"And I'm givin' you half," Archie said. "If'n you kin find it, that is."

"We couldn't take it," Matt said, shaking his head. "You worked hard for that gold."

"Means nothin'," Archie said, rolling down the window to spit. "Don't want it, but I hafta keep some, for if I git sick and hafta go t'the hospital." He stared out at the bobbing headlights of the old truck. "Woulda spent it all if it coulda saved Dorothy. We kept it 'cause she was sick and might need it, but she jist keeled over without warning. Never had a chance to use that gold to keep her well."

Adrienne glanced at him. "I don't know if you could have saved her. She had a bad heart, that's all."

"That's what she always said, too. Didn't want one of them transplants, either. Anyhow, I wish you'd take the danged gold," he muttered. "Dorothy'd want that."

Matt squeezed Adrienne's hand. "We'll see," he said. "We haven't found it yet."

"I think it might have something to do with Dorothy's books," Adrienne said. "Her riddle sounds like it's based on a Hans Christian Anderson fairy tale. Does she have a a book of fairy tales?"

"Might," Archie said, "but I looked in all her books. No gold."

"What if this is like a treasure hunt? What if there's a clue in the books that leads us to another clue, and so on?"

"That'd be jist like my ornery wife," Archie said. "She ain't never made anythin' easy fer me."

Adrienne chuckled. "When we get back, I'm looking for a book of fairy tales," Adrienne said. "I'll just bet there's another clue hidden there. We'll find that gold before you know it."

Matt pressed her hand against his thigh. "Let's hope so," he murmured.

Adrienne silently agreed with him. Gold was exciting, but so was the prospect of spending the night together somewhere. She didn't know how they'd manage it, but she was confident they would manage it, somehow.

Back at the cabin, Archie busied himself putting Dorothy into her stall and giving her some oats for her participation in the rescue.

"Help me find the book of fairy tales," Adrienne said, taking Matt's hand and leading him inside. Tonight lamps glowed in the living room, transforming the cabin into an inviting haven.

"If this starts looking like a wild-goose chase, I'm in favor of borrowing the truck again and searching out a place where we can stay tonight," Matt said.

"Let's give it an hour or so."

"That's a long time," Matt said, smiling at her. "Can you wait an hour?"

"Think of it this way. If we find the gold, you'll be able to afford to have your plane hauled out of the canyon and repaired."

"What about you? He said he was giving half to *us*, not just to me."

"If it wasn't for me, your plane wouldn't be down there in the first place."

"If I had airframe, or even hull insurance, we wouldn't need Archie's gold to get it out."

Adrienne gazed at him. It sounded as if he regretted his throw-caution-to-the-wind attitude. "Nevertheless, if we find the gold, I'm donating my share to getting that plane out. It's the least I can do."

"We'll see," Matt said. "Let's get started. I'll take the left side of the bookshelf and you take the right."

"Okay." She scanned the titles. Dorothy apparently had shelved the books by category. Adrienne found mostly nonfiction on her side, including books on nature, quilting, gourmet cooking, history and politics. Dorothy had been quite a scholar.

"This could be it," Matt said, handing her an open book with a scribbled note as a place marker.

Adrienne glanced at the title of the story. "'The Ugly Duckling.' I'm sure it is," she said, snatching the note. "Sure enough, here's a new riddle. Listen to this—Eloquent messenger, talented mime, capturing love, forever in time."

"Could it be another book? Books are messengers."

"Yes, but I don't think so. I don't think Dorothy would repeat herself like that."

Matt grinned. "You're starting to know her pretty well, aren't you?"

"Archie said we were alike," she admitted. "In fact, one of the reasons he wants us to have a share of the gold is that he thinks our relationship is similar to his and Dorothy's. He's sort of reliving it through us, I think."

Matt gazed at her. "Archie and Dorothy were married," he said quietly.

Her breathing quickened at the look in his eyes. "I know. Does that frighten you?"

"Not as much as snakes do," he said, winking at her. "Come on, Sherlock, let's solve this next clue. If it's not a book that's a messenger, what is it?"

Adrienne studied the short rhyme. "A messenger tells us something. And mimes use their hands...." She glanced slowly around the cabin. *"Forever in time,"* she murmured. "Wait! That's it. The next clue is in the ugly clock. I'd be willing to bet on it."

"Why the clock?"

"It's a messenger that uses hands, and it fits with *forever in time.* Besides, the clock was Archie's wedding present to Dorothy. He told me she always hated it, but he could never get her to take it down. He won't, either. That clock's a symbol of how much they cared for each other." She smiled triumphantly.

"Well, maybe."

"Don't you see the pattern?" Adrienne's excitement grew. "The first riddle was about appreciating an ugly duckling, who must be Archie. The second says that this object, the clock, captured the love he had for her, despite its homeliness."

Matt gazed at the clock. "It's really homely."

"But don't you see? As Dorothy learned to love him more, she didn't care if his gift was ugly, because he thought it was beautiful when he bought it for her. She was trying to tell him how much she loved him, and knew that he loved her, through these riddles."

"If you're right, there's another note in that clock. It isn't big enough to hold his cache."

"Grab a chair," Adrienne instructed. "We'll check it out."

Matt retrieved one of the ladder-back chairs from the kitchen, the same type they'd been tied to that morning, and placed it beneath the clock. He stood on the chair and was reaching for the clock when Archie came through the door.

"Git down!" Archie hollered. "Whatcha doin' with Dorothy's clock? Nobody touches that clock but me."

Matt nearly fell off the chair, but he righted himself and turned around. "We found another clue," he said. "Adrienne thinks it leads us to the clock."

"Horse feathers. Dorothy wouldn't leave no riddle in that clock. She hated that danged ugly thing."

"No, no she didn't," Adrienne said, going over to him and putting her hand on his arm. "Listen to this new riddle, Archie." She read the message again.

"Sounds familiar, somehow. But I don't git it," he said. "Jist like the first one. Dorothy made everything like that. Hard to unnerstand."

"Well, she was a scholar," Adrienne said. "And she liked to tease you, right?"

"Shore did! Ornery woman."

"But she loved all the things she used to tease you about, Archie. She loved that clock. She calls it an 'eloquent messenger' of your love for her."

Archie shifted his plug of tobacco to the other cheek. "Where'd you git this riddle?"

"It was in the book of fairy tales, marking the place of 'The Ugly Duckling.'"

"I done seen that!" Archie exploded, grabbing the paper from her. "I seen that in the book, and I thought it was one of them place markers. That's where I read them words before. Thought she copied it from one of them poetry books of hers."

"She wrote it for you, Archie."

He gazed at the slip of paper a moment longer and glanced away. Then he wiped his sleeve across his eyes.

"Can we look in the clock?" Adrienne asked gently.

"Reckon I'll look," Archie said.

Matt climbed down and steadied the chair while Archie heaved himself up.

He lifted the clock off the wall and stared at it for a long time. "You reckon she *liked* this danged thing?" he asked, glancing at Adrienne.

"I'm sure of it."

"Beats all," he said, shaking his head. "Beats all."

"Look in the back," Adrienne prompted.

Archie turned the clock over. "Nothin'."

Adrienne's shoulders sagged. "Are you sure?"

"Yep. No, wait. There's a tip of paper stickin' out. Never seed it before. All the danged times I set this clock, I never seed this." He pulled out the paper and unfolded it. He read the message silently, his lips moving. Then he hung the clock back carefully, adjusting it until it was straight, and climbed down from the chair.

"Well?" Matt asked.

"I git it now," he said, his voice husky. "You was right," he added, turning to Adrienne. "And I know where she done hid the gold."

11

Archie handed the piece of paper to Adrienne as he started out the door.

"What's it say?" Matt asked, crossing the room to peer over her shoulder.

Adrienne read the riddle aloud.

"Some women have ships to carry their name, others a child to widen their fame. A burro is mocked as tribute too small, but from you, my love t'was the greatest of all."

She looked up at Matt with tears in her eyes.

"That Dorothy was quite a lady."

"Yes, she was."

From the barn they heard a loud braying.

"Guess we'd better get out there," Matt said, guiding Adrienne toward the door. "Archie's tearing apart Dorothy the third's home and she doesn't appear to like it much."

They hurried through the chill night air toward the barn, where light from the kerosene lamp spilled out into the yard. Dorothy the third's brays continued to rend the stillness, punctuated with Archie's commands for her to shut up for once in her life.

When they entered the barn they discovered the burro tied up in the bare stall, away from the oats she'd been eating, and a flurry of straw arcing out of the stall where Archie was shoveling furiously. "Shoulda knowed she'd put it somewhere like this," he muttered. "Right after I put clean straw down and a new burro in here. Shoulda knowed it. Ornery woman."

Adrienne walked over to the burro and laid her hand on its soft neck. "Take it easy," she crooned. "You'll have plenty of oats when this is over." The burro flicked her ears forward and looked at Adrienne with her large brown eyes. "That's it," Adrienne soothed, stroking her neck and scratching between her ears. "You have a good home here, the best. Archie loves you very much. No need to get all excited over a few lost oats." Adrienne heard a chuckle and glanced up.

Matt leaned against the stall and watched her with amusement. "Amazing," he said. "I couldn't picture it before, the stockbroker who used to be a 4-H girl. Seeing you with that burro, that image comes into focus."

"And?"

"It's a nice image," he said, "and I take back all the crummy things I said about your horse. I'm sure it was as important for you to get back to Granny as if she'd been a human being."

Adrienne returned his gaze as she continued to scratch Dorothy the third's ears. "Thanks," she said, smiling back. "How come you're not watching Archie tear up the floor?"

"I'd rather watch you."

A flutter began in her stomach. If they located the gold, then soon they could leave. Soon they could be in each other's arms. Soon . . .

"Matt, hand me that there crowbar, will ya?" Archie called out.

Matt turned and rummaged through the tools on the shelf behind him until he found the crowbar. He handed it over the mound of straw to Archie, who was kneeling in the stall. "How do you know which boards to pry up?" he asked.

"The dang woman did one thing right," Archie replied, wedging the crowbar under a plank. "She done put a tiny X over this here board. I missed it before, 'cause I didn't know t'look."

Matt laughed. "X marks the spot. So this was a treasure hunt, after all."

"Yep," Archie said, prying at the board. "Jist like Dorothy. Loved puzzles. Loved them crosswords. Jist like her."

"Want some help with that crowbar?"

"Thank y'kindly, but you folks did the brain work. Least I can do is dig it up. I'm good fer that."

Adrienne gave the burro one last pat and walked around the end of the stall to watch Archie. "You're good for a lot of things, Archie. You've kept the place up beautifully since . . . since you lost Dorothy."

Archie wrenched at the board. "Didn't lose her. Know right where she is." He heaved again and nearly fell over as the board came up with a groaning sound. He tossed it aside and peered into the opening. "Yep," he said, and started to laugh. "This shore is the place. That ornery woman." He picked a piece of paper from the opening. He scanned it silently and passed it back to Adrienne.

She held it so that Matt could read Dorothy's last words.

Your earthly treasure is buried here beneath the floor, but we must bury the treasure of our love no more. You are my world. Let's not fight.

Love,
Dorothy

Adrienne stepped forward and put her hand on Archie's shoulder. His grizzly head was bent as he stared vacantly at the hole in the floor. "She really loved you," Adrienne said. "Her riddles tell you that. She thought you'd solve them, or the two of you would solve them together, and you'd know how much she cared."

He nodded slowly.

Adrienne knew that Dorothy's riddles and the messages of love meant more to him than the gold he'd uncovered. Yet as the discovery dawned more fully upon Adrienne, she began to wonder if Archie really intended to give them, or more precisely Matt, half of it. If so, she hoped there would be enough to salvage the plane.

Growing more curious, she stood on tiptoe and looked into the hole. Light from the kerosene lamp illuminated the turquoise top of three Skippy Peanut Butter jars. Adrienne had expected a leather pouch with a drawstring, like in the movies. "You put your gold in peanut butter jars?" she asked.

"Yep." Archie sighed and wiped his sleeve across his eyes. "Might as well take 'em out, now. Dorothy didn't mean fer me to leave 'em in there. This'n can be yers, you and Matt, and one fer me, and we'll split up the last one."

Adrienne took the jar eagerly, but when she held it up to look through the glass, she felt sick with disappointment. The jar contained a blackish mix of sand and particles of various sizes, from just flecks to peppercorn size. It wasn't gold, but some junk that Archie had dug up, perhaps convincing himself that it was gold, perhaps convincing Dorothy, too.

She glanced at Matt. "I'm sorry," she murmured. "I had hoped you'd get the plane out."

"I most definitely will," he said, staring at the jar.

She backed away from Archie and motioned for Matt to follow. When he joined her, she lowered her voice. "This isn't gold. He's convinced himself it is, and if you want to take half, to humor him, then I understand, but—"

Matt began to laugh. "What would you estimate three peanut butter jars like those are worth?"

"Nothing, unless you recycle the glass. Then maybe a few cents."

"Try fifty or sixty thousand."

"Dollars?" Adrienne cried, and clapped her hand over her mouth. She glanced over at Archie, who had turned to grin at her.

"She don't think that there's gold, do she?" he asked.

"But it can't be!" Adrienne exclaimed. "It's all sand, and funny little pieces of rock, and it doesn't glitter or anything."

"If'n it glittered, you'd best not be solvin' riddles to find it. T'ain't worth nothin' if it glitters." He took the other two jars out and stood up. "Glitterin' stuff is fool's gold," he added, spitting into the pail nearby.

Adrienne held the jar up and peered at it. "This is really gold?"

"Shore is."

"I would have thrown these jars in the garbage if I'd found them."

Matt laughed again. "Good thing you weren't in charge."

"How do *you* know so much about this?"

"My dad's always been fascinated with prospecting. Showed me what he found once, a tiny sample of what's in these jars. I think it's called 'concentrate.' That right, Archie?"

Archie nodded.

"Anyway, I thought it was junk, too, but my dad soon convinced me otherwise. In fact, he tried to get me to go out with him, but I never did."

"Because of the snakes," Adrienne guessed.

"You got it."

Once more Adrienne looked at the contents of the jar she held before handing it to Matt. "This is yours."

"No, this is Archie's." Matt turned back to the gray-haired man and held the jar out to him. "You're very generous to offer, but we can't take your life savings, or even part of it."

Archie stood there, looking uncertain. "Maybe I didn't say it right. This here is from me to you folks, because ever' young couple needs a start. Me'n Dorothy, we had a start from her mother, who left us a little pile of money. Dorothy would want me t'help. I know she would."

Matt glanced at Adrienne. "That's very nice of you, Archie, but Adrienne and I—well, we haven't exactly—"

"Set the date? Aw, shucks, that won't be no time at all. I kin tell by how you make those calf-eyes. You two is jist rarin' t'git at each other."

Adrienne blushed at the accuracy of his assessment. Of course, he was an old-fashioned guy, who assumed that two people who were "rarin' t'git at each other" had plans to marry and needed a nest egg. She'd wanted the money for Matt's plane, but if he felt uncomfortable accepting it, she understood and would support him. They'd find another way to get the plane out. "Matt's right, Archie," she said, speaking gently. "We wouldn't feel right taking your gold."

The old man glanced from one to the other with a crestfallen expression. "Dang it. Dorothy always said I didn't know nothin' about presents. Said I didn't do it right. I musta said somethin' wrong."

"Oh, no you didn't," Adrienne cried, going to him and putting her hand on his arm. "It's just that—" She paused and looked back at Matt with a silent plea for assistance. He looked as upset as she felt. In turning down the gold, they'd hurt Archie's feelings.

"I ain't got much to be joyful about," Archie said. "Since you two been here, I had a little more joy, watchin' you fight, watchin' you make up. Put me so much in mind of me'n Dorothy, I felt like she was back. I jist . . ." He glanced away. "I jist want t'hold on t'that joy. If'n you took some of the gold, I'd still be hitched up, somehow. I'd be part of your future, even if'n I never seed you agin."

Matt stepped forward and put one arm around Adrienne and the other around Archie. "Then we'll take half," he said, his voice rough with emotion. "And you'll see us again, Archie. After all this, we're sort of like family, aren't we?"

Archie looked at him, his eyes moist. "Sorta like. Wanna have a drink on it?"

Matt looked to Adrienne for a reaction, and when she nodded, he smiled. "Sure," he said.

"You know, I didn't generally drink so much, when Dorothy was alive," Archie said. He looked down at the two peanut butter jars he held. "Maybe I won't drink so much now, neither, knowin' how Dorothy— how she, well, felt about me and all."

"We understand," Adrienne said, giving him a hug.

"Besides, if'n you come t'visit, one day you'll be bringin' youngins, and you can't be bringin' 'em to see some drunk old man."

Adrienne stepped back. These assumptions were getting out of hand. "Well, I—"

"In due time," Archie said, grinning at her. "You folks ain't hardly been alone to figure these things out. Always had somebody hangin' around, like me, or them two skunks Curtis and Jeb." He turned to Matt. "Which puts me in mind of somethin'. You two oughta press charges against them skunks."

"I'd planned to," Matt said, "once everything settled down. I'd love to settle my score with them personally, but filing charges is probably better. I'll—"

"Matt—" Adrienne interrupted, touching his arm, "let it go."

"After the way they treated you?" Matt frowned. "No way."

"Please. We'd have to testify against them, and I'd rather we didn't ever have to see them again."

Matt gazed at her. "I don't want to put you through any more agony on their account, but something should be done."

"I have me a thought," Archie said. "Reckon I could put in a call to the sheriff, tell him what Jeb and Curtis done. The sheriff'll probably put them two on curfew agin."

"Curfew?" Matt asked.

"Yep. Last time they wasn't allowed out after ten at night fer six months. Maybe this time'll be longer."

Matt laughed. "Maybe that's the answer."

"I got me another idea," Archie said, gazing at Matt. "Mrs. Potter, friend of mine, runs this here bed-and-breakfast place in Saddlehorn. Won't nobody be there this time of year." Archie spat into the pail before winking slyly at Matt. "Would ya like t'know the whereabouts of that there bed-and-breakfast?"

Matt glanced at Adrienne. "Point me in the right direction, Archie," he said.

WITHIN HALF AN HOUR Adrienne had bid Archie a tearful farewell and was driving with Matt in the old truck toward Saddlehorn. They'd arranged that Matt would put her on a bus for Tucson the following morning. Then he'd return and supervise the salvaging of his plane.

Adrienne sniffled a few more times and blew her nose. "That old man really got to me."

"Me, too." Matt put his arm around her and pulled her closer on the old seat.

"Matt, since you'll be at Archie's for several days, maybe you can gently straighten him out about our relationship. He's already expecting us to bring our children out to see him."

Matt glanced down at her with an expression she couldn't read. "I'll straighten him out," he said. Then he released his hold on her and put both hands on the steering wheel.

"What? What did I say?"

"Only what you've been saying all along, that you don't want to get permanently tangled up with me. I should have understood the message by now."

"That's not what I meant! I *do* want to get tangled up with you."

He took his attention from the road for a brief second. "Oh? In what way?"

"Well, I—" She paused, not sure herself what she wanted. "I think we have a . . . a chance for a relationship, but after all, we've known each other a very short time. We need to get acquainted, to learn—"

"Bull."

"I beg your pardon?"

"Oh, God. Now we're back to 'I beg your pardon.' Adrienne, after the past twenty-four hours, anything about me you *don't* know is unimportant. Ditto for what I don't know about you. We've communicated on a gut level of sheer survival. We've learned how to work together, how to fight, how to make up, how to love each other." He slammed on the brakes. "I love you, dammit! What else is there?"

She stared at him, openmouthed. "You've never said that," she whispered.

"I've been a little busy, okay?" He turned off the ignition and faced her. "I've been a little busy with plane crashes, and gunpowder, and guys with double-barreled shotguns, and snakes, and ropes that might unravel, and hunting for gold, and saving your precious behind!"

"And I appreciate it!"

"Then how come I have to be the one to break the ice? How come I have to be the first to say it, and then you wonder why I've never said it before, huh?"

"Okay! I love you, too!"

"Good!" He swiveled in his seat and started the truck. "Then let's get on with it."

They sat in silence, on opposite sides of the truck. Adrienne stared at the lonely road and wondered if they'd truly just confessed their love for each other. Then she heard a muffled sound from Matt's side of the truck. Eventually she realized he was laughing, and she began to grin. She glanced at him. "Typical, huh?"

"I tell you, Burnham, I still don't know what it's going to be between you and me, but as Archie would say, it' ain't gonna be dull. Now come on back over here."

"Are you sure you should drive one-handed?"

Matt sighed. "I should have known you'd say that. Listen, if I can drive with the barrel of a gun in my crotch, I can drive with my arm around you, although sometimes I wonder if you're not more dangerous than a loaded gun."

"That's how Jeb made you drive, with the barrel of a gun in your lap?"

"He did."

She scooted under his arm. "Oh, Matt, I had no idea."

"Are you going to make it up to me?"

"If I can." She slipped her hand over the denim of his thigh.

He drew in a sharp breath. "I most definitely think you can."

They drove down the main street of Saddlehorn and passed the bar where Curtis's truck was parked. Just then a sheriff's car pulled in beside the truck.

Matt grinned. "I think curfew time has arrived," he said.

"They both deserve that and more," Adrienne said with feeling. "Especially that Curtis. Ugh."

Matt's tone was conversational. "If he'd done anything to you, I would have killed him."

"I believe you really would have," Adrienne said, shivering.

"So do I, and trust me, I'm not the murdering type. But when he started on the buttons of your blouse—"

"It was horrible, Matt."

"Yes, it was. I'm sorry I brought it up. We have better things to think about," he added, turning down a dark unpaved lane. "The bed-and-breakfast should be at the end of this road."

"I can hardly believe there is such a place, and that we really can . . ."

Matt chuckled. "Oh, yes, we can. And we will."

Adrienne tingled with anticipation. Ahead of them a single porch light shone as a beacon. Archie had mentioned that Mrs. Potter kept her porch light on to guide her guests. They parked in front of a two-story Victorian structure freshly painted yellow with white gingerbread trim.

"What will we say?" Adrienne asked as Matt helped her out of the driver's side of the cab. "We don't have luggage, and we're not married. Maybe she won't—"

"We'll say that Archie sent us."

A woman in her mid-sixties answered the door.

"Are you Mrs. Potter?" Matt asked.

"Yes," the woman replied.

"We'd like a room, if you have one," Matt said solemnly, although theirs was the only vehicle in sight.

"I do have a vacancy," the woman said, looking them over. "Would an upstairs corner room suit?"

Matt turned to Adrienne. "Is the second floor too high for you?"

She smiled sweetly into his face but she reached behind him and pinched his bottom through the denim. "I can manage," she said, satisfied when he gave a startled yelp.

"Where are you folks from?" the woman asked, peering beyond them to Archie's truck. "Seems like I know that vehicle."

"Archie sent us," Matt said.

"Oh." That seemed to make everything all right. "Well come in, come in. Any bags?"

"No," Adrienne said. "We hadn't expected to be staying overnight in Saddlehorn, but we—there have been a few complications."

"No matter," Mrs. Potter said. "Is there anything you need? Anybody who's a friend of Archie's is a friend of mine."

"I think we're fine," Adrienne said. "I understand there's a bus that comes through Saddlehorn in the morning?"

"Yes, at ten-fifteen." Mrs. Potter gazed at her. "How is Archie? I've been worried about him ever since Dorothy died."

"I think Archie's better now," Adrienne said. "While we were there he found a message from her, one she'd written before she died. I think the message comforted him."

"Oh, that's wonderful. It was pure fate that they met. She stopped at the café on her way through town and Archie happened to be there. He fell for her like a ton of bricks, and she took to him right away, too. Seemed to like the fact he was older than her. She told me once she thought her poor health would cheat a younger man."

"They really loved each other, didn't they?" Adrienne said.

"Yes, although a stranger might not have thought so. They were always fighting."

"So we hear," Matt said.

"He must think a lot of you two," Mrs. Potter continued, "if he loaned you his truck. He doesn't often do that. May never have done that, come to think of it."

Matt nodded. "We know. He sort of adopted us after we—well, it's a long story."

"And you'd like to get some rest, I'll bet."

"Yes," Matt said, not looking at Adrienne. "Yes, we would."

"Then I'll show you up to your room as soon as we take care of a few bookkeeping details. How would you like to pay for this?"

Adrienne and Matt spoke in unison. "I'll handle it," they said together, and then stared at each other.

"Look," Matt said, "let me get it. You've already turned over all the . . . the contents of the peanut butter jar to me. The least I can do is—"

"Matt Kirkland, that's how you got in this jam in the first place, by not conserving your resources. You may need every penny to salvage that plane."

He glared at her. "This is as important as salvaging my plane."

Mrs. Potter glanced from one to the other as they argued. "Would you like me to split the bill?" she asked.

"No!" Adrienne and Matt said together.

Then Matt smiled at the woman. "Pardon us. We need a brief conference," he said, as he guided Adrienne a few feet away. "Are we going to fight about this, too?" he asked.

"Even though we're not talking about a large amount of money, I think that you have to learn fiscal responsibility, Matt. Otherwise your business will never be on sound footing. This is the very sort of impulsive move that—" Her lecture ended when he pulled her into his arms and kissed her.

The kiss was hard, swift, and effective. "Will you allow me to pay for this night of sinful pleasure?" he murmured, gazing into her eyes. "Or do you plan to waste more time debating economics?"

"Matt, this is embarrassing," she whispered, even as her body molded to his and her pulse raced.

He rubbed the small of her back. "Will you give up the fight?"

"Yes, but this is no way to settle things."

"Isn't it?" With another quick kiss he released her and walked over to Mrs. Potter. "Put our bill on this," he said, taking a credit card from his wallet. "Sorry about the delay."

The woman laughed and walked over to a rolltop desk. "I think I understand what Archie sees in you two. You argue just the way he and Dorothy did."

"We've been told that," he turned around to wink at Adrienne, and she made a face at him. He chuckled.

The woman took an imprint of Matt's card and asked him to sign. Then she led them upstairs to their room, and with a smile, she left them alone.

It was the most flower- and lace-filled decorating scheme Adrienne had ever seen. Roses in all colors and types covered the wallpaper, the comforter, the canopy over the king-sized four-poster, and the towels in the adjoining bathroom. Where the roses ended, the lace trim began.

She walked to the foot of the bed and gazed at the expanse of flowers. A wealth of lacy, bow-decked toss pillows nearly obscured the headboard. Adrienne could imagine what a man like Matt would think of such frippery. She turned as Matt closed the door. "I suppose you don't care for this room."

He leaned against the door frame and crossed his arms. "As I stand here I can imagine all sorts of things we can argue about, Burnham. The flowery junk is one, who gets which side of the bed is another, whether the window will be closed or open a crack is another, how to squeeze the toothpaste Archie gave us is one more. Shall I go on?"

She was drawn in by the picture he made. He still wore the rust-colored shirt, jeans and boots Archie had loaned him. She admired the broad shoulders and strong arms that had kept her from harm's way so often in the past twenty-four hours. Dust from their escapade in the canyon clung to the denim that hugged his hips, and mud still smeared his boots. Because he looked so out of place as he leaned against the pristine white of the door, surrounded on all sides by lace and roses, he also looked more masculine than she ever remembered.

He uncrossed his arms and moved toward her. Instinctively she backed up, but the foot of the bed prevented her from going any farther.

"I could tell you I don't give a damn about any of those things," he said, "but you'd find something else to fight about, I'm sure."

She caught his scent now, the faint whiff of aftershave mingled with something musky and elemental. "You make me sound so combative," she said.

"You? How could I have gotten that idea?" As he advanced, he pulled open the front of his shirt and the snaps gave way with the sound of corn popping. "I'm sure when you were born you told the doctor how he might have improved his technique. You probably instructed him on how to pat that delicious, bare bottom of yours."

She hadn't seen him in full light before. Passion robbed her of speech as she watched the steady rise and fall of his muscled chest, his dusky nipples half-hidden within a swirling pattern of dark brown hair. She'd never wanted a man as much as she wanted him, and the urgency frightened her.

"I figure you have an opinion about how I should make love to you," he added, flinging the shirt aside, "and how I should undress you, and in what order I should kiss certain parts of you." He stood half an arm's reach from her now. "If so, you'd better tell me now."

She trembled as he unfastened the first button of her blouse.

"Go ahead," he continued, moving through the task with deliberate motions. "Tell me this isn't the right way, and then we can fight about it, if you want. We can argue right up to the final moment, but know this—there will be a final moment."

She moistened her dry lips with her tongue. Her heart pounded so loud she thought he must be able to hear.

Coolly, seemingly without emotion, he tugged her blouse free of her jeans. "I don't care if twenty desperadoes are pounding on the door, or a tornado comes through Saddlehorn, or the damn house catches fire. After what we've been through, I figure anything might happen." He tossed the blouse aside.

She gazed into the hazel depths of his eyes. She could not have moved if her life had been at stake.

"Just so you know what to expect, Burnham," he said softly, "nothing, and I mean nothing, will stop me from loving the living daylights out of you tonight."

12

ADRIANNE REACHED UP and locked her hands behind his neck. "I always knew you were a cocky son-of-a-gun," she managed, her voice husky.

"Confident."

"So prove it, fly-boy."

"You bet," he murmured, crushing her against him.

She met his passion head-on, pushing herself shamelessly against him and parting her lips to welcome the thrust of his tongue. When he slipped his hands beneath her camisole, she raised her arms so that he could slide it off. With the camisole gone, he filled his hands with her lushness and leaned down to savor the delights that he held.

Head thrown back she was momentarily off balance. She reached blindly for the bedpost and grasped it to steady herself. Still tasting her breasts, he slipped an arm around her waist and gently removed her hand from the post.

"Trust me, Adrienne," he whispered, his breath warm against her damp skin. "I won't let you fall. You're safe, Adrienne. Safe with me."

She closed her eyes and relaxed in his arms, knowing it was true, knowing she could allow this drenching desire to take over, because he would be there. Gradually he guided her downward until she lay against the plump quilting of the comforter. On his knees beside her, he reached down and slipped off her moccasins. She opened her eyes and looked up as he hovered over her, framed by a canopy of flowers.

"I love you," he said, clearly, distinctly. No mumbled declaration. He meant this to be heard.

She touched his cheek. "I know."

"More than this, more than what we're about to do."

She couldn't doubt it, not after all he'd risked for her. "I know that, too."

"But, oh, how I want you," he said, stroking the back of his hand down the valley between her breasts. "It's as if we've waited years for a night like this."

"We have," she murmured. "All our lives."

Recognition glowed in his eyes. "That's true."

Clasping his hand, she held it against her thudding heart. "And I love you," she said, just as clearly as he had.

"I know. I can see it in your eyes. Such beautiful brown eyes."

"Make love to me," she whispered. "I want you. Every bit as much as you want me."

He smiled as he gently released the catch on her jeans. "That point could be argued."

"But you won't."

"No," he whispered, leaning over to capture her lips as he slowly drew the zipper of her jeans down. His kiss, in turn commanding and cajoling, involved her senses so thoroughly that she hardly realized he'd removed the rest of her clothes. When his fingers found her, she moaned and clutched at his shoulders. For his touch there, in that very spot, she would give all she owned and count it a bargain.

He lifted his lips from hers and gazed into her eyes. "I'm glad for all the hell we've been through," he said, stroking her slowly until she writhed with pleasure. "It makes this so much sweeter."

"Yes," she said, her breath coming in short gasps. "Oh, Matt . . ." She arched against the heel of his hand.

"And we've only begun," he murmured, kneeling at the foot of the bed and moving between her thighs. He kissed the smooth curve of her stomach down to her flaxen curls. "I've waited for this, for everything that is you, for you to risk being vulnerable to me."

As if she had a choice. His warm breath against her skin brought such a rush of untamed passion that she yearned for his intimate kiss. When he bestowed it, she cried out for joy and tangled her fingers through his hair.

He loved her so exquisitely that she thought she might die of pleasure, and she told him so, in gasping praise as her world spun into a kaleidoscope of rose petals. Then with slow, lingering kisses, he drew away, and through her haze of sensation she realized he was discarding the rest of his clothes. A rip of cellophane. He was taking care of her, of them, again.

She felt his breath on her face, the weight of his hands braced on either side of her head. She opened her eyes. "No desperadoes pounding at the door," she whispered, smiling.

"No tornadoes."

"Nothing to stop us."

His hazel eyes glittered. "Nothing on earth."

"Then come to me," she said, and arched up to meet him. They joined as if completing the last piece of a puzzle, as if they'd found the only perfect fit in all the world.

"Yes," Matt groaned, closing his eyes.

Yes, answered her heart. This man was her mate, the one for a lifetime. She must never let him go. Never. She held him tight as he began to move inside her.

He opened his eyes and gazed at her as he increased the rhythm. "This is right, so right," he said, his breathing ragged. "I knew it would be. I knew... Adrienne, oh, Adrienne, hold on. Hold on, my love."

"I love you," she cried, as the tension mounted. She wrapped her legs around him and he moaned as he thrust deeper.

As the pulse of her quickening became stronger, he seemed to sense it and matched himself to her response. "Now," he murmured. "Now, now!"

She surged against him as wave after wave of sensation cascaded over her in time with his shudders. They were one, never to be torn asunder. He sank slowly down and rested his cheek against her breast. She held his head and closed her eyes. At last, at long last she was sure.

THEIR POSITION WAS too cramped and cold to hold for long; Matt retreated to the bathroom, and Adrienne got rid of the toss pillows, threw back the bedspread and discovered two king-sized goose-down pillows. The cases and sheets were as densely covered with roses as the rest of the decor was. Still, the bed was comfortable and she sighed as she stretched out and pulled the sheet and comforter over her.

Matt returned and picked up his jeans.

"Getting dressed?" she asked, enjoying the unclothed beauty of him.

"Nope." He reached in the pocket and pulled out several small packages all alike. "Getting supplies."

"You think we might do that again, do you?" She tingled at the thought of welcoming him inside her once more.

"I think we just might. Especially if I can find you," he said, tossing the packages on the bedside table and climbing under the covers. "As pink and rosy as you are, I might lose track of you in this seed catalog Mrs. Potter calls a bedroom."

She propped herself on her elbow. "I knew you didn't like it."

"Wrong. I love it. We should probably have our bedroom decorated this way, to remind us."

"*Our* bedroom? We don't have one."

"Yet." He pulled her close and planted soft kisses all over her face. "Marry me, Adrienne. Make love to me in a room full of roses for the rest of our lives."

"Yes," she sighed, nestling closer. "Of course I'll marry you."

"You will?" He pulled back to stare at her in surprise. "I thought for sure I'd get an argument out of you, at least at first."

"What would you like to argue about?"

"I wouldn't *like* to argue. I just thought, considering the way our relationship has gone, that you'd want to discuss a whole bunch of stuff before you made this decision."

"No, I don't." The place he had in her heart would never change. She wanted to marry this man; never in her life had she been so certain of anything.

"But you've only known me for a little while." He sounded perplexed. "Wait a minute. That's supposed to be your line, not mine."

She smiled. "You said *we* crammed a lifetime into these past few hours. You said I already know all I need to know."

"Well . . . well, that's right." He thought some more and then narrowed his eyes. "Long engagement or short?"

"Short."

"Big wedding or small?"

"Small."

"Damn. I can't get used to this. Those are the choices *I'd* make."

She laughed. "Are you disappointed we don't have anything to fight about?"

He flopped back on the pillow. "Let's just say I'm nervous. Nothing's been this easy with you."

"Nothing?" she teased, sliding her hand beneath the covers to caress him.

"Well, maybe one thing."

"Perhaps we're turning over a new leaf," she said. "Maybe we'll have smooth sailing from here on out."

He closed his eyes and sighed. "Keep touching me like that and I'll believe anything you say."

"Then believe this—I love you and plan to have a beautiful life with you. Everything will work out. You'll see."

Matt rolled on his side and wrapped her in his arms. "Burnham, you have a most convincing manner. In fact, with a manner like yours, we may never fight again." Then he claimed a kiss as he began loving her all over again.

A LIGHT TAPPING on the bedroom door woke Adrienne from a sound sleep. Matt was tucked against her. Sunlight sifting around the edges of the flowered curtains told her it was well past dawn. She eased out of bed and Matt didn't stir. Grabbing a large towel from the bathroom, she wrapped herself in it before going to the door. "Yes?" she called softly.

"Breakfast is here," called Mrs. Potter. "I thought that if you wanted to catch that bus, you'd need to be getting up."

"Oh. Thank you. What time is it?"

"Eight-thirty. I'll set the tray out here by the door for you. The muffins are hot and homemade."

"Thank you. Thank you very much." Adrienne waited until she heard the woman descend the stairs before she opened the door and bent to reach the tray.

"Now that's a picture," Matt said from behind her.

She whirled and the towel fell off.

"And that's an even nicer one." His head and shoulders were propped against the headboard and he was watching her.

"Fine thing," she said, closing the door and retrieving the towel. "I'm trying to get your breakfast without wandering in the hall stark naked, and you make fun of me." She wrapped the towel around herself again and tucked the end in securely.

"That wasn't making fun. That was paying my deepest respects. Go ahead. I want to see you bend over to pick up the tray."

"Oh, really?" She sashayed back to the bed and deliberately unhooked the towel. It fell to the floor as she eased onto the bed and crawled slowly toward him. She noticed his gaze fixed on her swaying breasts. She smiled. "I think maybe I'd like to be served breakfast in bed," she said, leaning down and allowing her breasts to brush against him. "Think you could manage to get the tray?"

"Not in my present condition."

"But you could use a towel," she whispered, nibbling at his lower lip.

"To go with the towel rack I'm developing?" he said, grabbing her and rolling her to her back. "You think you're pretty smart, don't you?"

"Yes," she said, laughing.

"Well, you're not so smart," he said, stripping away the covers, "because your breakfast is going to be cold."

SOME TIME LATER Matt dragged on his jeans and brought the tray in. The blueberry muffins were cold, but the coffee, kept in a carafe, was still steaming hot.

"I may prefer cold muffins from now on," Matt said, licking crumbs from his fingers. They sat at a small table in two straight-backed chairs that were either antiques or good copies of antiques. Matt wore only his jeans and Adrienne had wrapped herself in the comforter.

"Maybe you'll even want to live in Saddlehorn," she suggested.

"Not unless Jeb and Curtis move and somebody builds an airstrip."

Adrienne cradled her coffee cup and took another sip of the warm brew while she admired the picture Matt made sitting across from her. She could grow quite fond of drinking her morning coffee while watching the play of muscles across his bare chest.

He smiled at her. "You look happy."

"I am."

"I know. You love me for my gold."

She laughed. "Nope. But speaking of that, I have an idea. Let's say your share of Archie's gold is twenty-five or thirty thousand. Let's say twenty-five, to be on the conservative side."

"Why not say thirty-five to be on the extravagant side?"

She glanced at him.

"Just kidding," he said, holding up his hand. "You should see the expression on your face, though, Burnham. The word *prune* comes to mind."

"Well, I'm trying to have a serious discussion with you."

"Dressed in a flowered comforter, that's not too easy."

"Don't think of me that way. Think of me in a business suit in my office."

"I'd rather think of you in absolutely nothing in my bed."

"Matt, come on, now. I'm a professional investment counselor. Let me counsel you."

He gazed at her and a wary look came into his eyes. "Okay," he said slowly, and put down his coffee cup.

She ignored the look. He'd see that her suggestion had merit, once he'd heard her out. "How much of the twenty-five thousand will you use to salvage the plane and repair it?"

"I'm not sure. A good chunk, maybe, considering where it is. Although the body is in fair shape, I think there was all sorts of damage to the engine, not to mention whatever caused it to conk out in the first place."

"Well, a rough estimate, then," she said.

"Let's just say that I'm counting on not having it run over twenty-five, which is what I think Archie's gold is worth."

She leaned her arms on the table and gazed at him. "Matt, you'll be right back where you started."

"Yeah. Pretty lucky, huh?" He smiled at her. "Well, not *right* back where I started," he added, leaning over and tracing a line along her bare forearm. "In the most important respect I'm way ahead."

She caught his hand and laced her fingers through his. "You could be ahead in *all* respects."

The wary look returned. "How?"

"Sell the plane."

"*Sell* it? You're kidding."

Adrienne shook her head. "Find the cheapest way to haul the pieces out, sell the parts as is, and invest the rest of your share of Archie's money. I even have some ideas of where to invest. Information came in Friday on some securities that—"

"Wait a minute." He untangled his fingers and withdrew his hand from hers. "Then I wouldn't have a plane. I couldn't start my business."

"You shouldn't have started it in the first place. You were undercapitalized. You couldn't afford the insurance to cover your investment, that A-frame thing."

He frowned and shifted in his chair. "That's airframe, not A-frame."

"Whatever. But now you have another chance. Let me work with your money, build it up a little more before you leap into this venture, so when you buy your next plane, you'll be on better financial footing."

He stared at her. "And how long would that take?"

"I'm not sure. First we have to see how much capital you have after selling the plane, and what the market is doing. You can't be impatient with investments, but in time you'd—"

"Weeks? Months?"

Adrienne shook her head. "Longer than that, of course. Matt, surely after what's happened, you see the risks of what you did. I would think that the crash would have taught you that you need to proceed more cautiously."

He shoved his coffee cup back and stood up. "And I would have thought this weekend would have taught you the exact opposite."

"And what's that supposed to mean?" she shot back, her retort a conditioned reflex. Then she wanted to take back the words and change her tone of voice. Her stomach began to hurt. Their arguments before had been a challenge, sometimes almost fun, but not this time. She didn't want to have this fight. The stakes were too high.

He paced across the small room and turned back to her. "It means that you have to grab life as it comes by," he said, grasping at the air and making a tight fist. "Because you don't know what's around the corner, or how long you'll be around to enjoy being alive. Good God, after all we've been through, how can you talk about taking the safe path?"

"And how can you not?" She wrapped the comforter around her and stood, too. "You nearly lost everything. Don't you want to guard against that happening again?"

"I know that security's an illusion. I know that you can be on the brink of disaster and suddenly everything turns around for you, like this, like Archie's gold. And that happens to me all the time! I have this knack for coming out ahead. With a break like getting half the gold, I'd be a fool not to repair that plane and begin my flight school. I'd be a fool not to grab my chance!"

Adrienne swallowed, trying to remove the bitter taste from her mouth. Matt hadn't changed. Perhaps if Archie hadn't produced fifty or sixty thousand dollars worth of gold, Matt would have understood that you can't always bounce back from disaster. But they had Archie's gold, and he thought that was evidence that his good luck charm was still working, would always work. She didn't believe in good luck charms. She believed in careful planning.

She drew the comforter more tightly around her but still she trembled with cold. She tried twice to begin the sentence that burned like dry ice in her mind. On the third try she choked out the words. "I can't marry a man who thinks like that."

13

PAIN FLASHED through Matt's hazel eyes. Then a resigned expression came over his face. "That's what I've been expecting you to say all along. I was afraid all this sweetness and light was too good to be true."

"After everything that's happened, I thought you'd be different!"

"And I thought you'd be different!" he shouted back. "I guess we both expected a miracle to happen, like in the movies, and we'd each become the person the other one wanted. Well, this isn't the movies."

"Matt," she begged, tears swimming in her eyes, "can't you see that—"

"No, I can't." His voice sounded hoarse. "I can't see me living by your prissy rules. And apparently you don't approve of the way I handle things, so it's a wash."

"But I love you."

"Do you? Love doesn't try to fit people into a mold."

"Love doesn't behave recklessly where others are concerned, either!"

He gazed at her, and the silence beat upon her ears more than the shouting. "You call me reckless?" he asked softly. "The person who a few hours ago said she'd marry me, and now has changed her mind?"

Adrienne choked back a sob. "I guess I've been around you too long."

Pain etched his features again. "We can fix that," he said, turning away. "Saddlehorn's a small place," he said, retrieving his shirt and his boots. "When you need to find the bus stop, just ask anyone. I'm sure they can direct you."

"You're leaving?" Tears streamed down her cheeks and dripped onto the flowered comforter wrapped around her shoulders.

"Might as well." He tucked in his shirt and sat on the bed to pull on his boots. Then he slipped his wallet into his back pocket. "You obviously don't need me," he said, and walked out the door without looking back.

THE COMBINATION OF SHOCK and exhaustion kept Adrienne numb through the long bus ride back to Tucson. She'd called her roommate Margaret from Saddlehorn and Margaret had met her at the Greyhound depot and bundled her home to bed.

Adrienne hadn't told Margaret the whole story until the next day. That same day she broke off her relationship with Alex.

That night the roommates shared a pizza Margaret had insisted on buying to save them both the work of cooking. Seated at their kitchen table, Adrienne studied her friend. Margaret's skin was tanned and her short, curly brown hair was sun-bleached from hours spent in their apartment building's heated outdoor pool.

Margaret taught high school physical education. Adrienne had met her two years ago by answering

Margaret's newspaper ad requesting a roommate. Adrienne often thought that she and Margaret couldn't have chosen better if they'd had a hundred years to search. It was the only other time in her life Adrienne had made a hasty decision. Agreeing to marry Matt had obviously pushed what little luck she had too far.

"I don't get it," Margaret said, opening the pizza box and extracting a slice. "If this guy Matt isn't right because he's too irresponsible, why dump Alex, the most responsible man in the universe?"

"I had to break up with Alex," Adrienne said, "because he cornered me in the hall at work today and tried to kiss me."

"He probably missed you. He was upset when I told him he couldn't come over to see you last night. Still, I guess that's not too cool, having a guy grab you when you're trying to act like a professional."

"It wasn't the professional part that bothered me, although I didn't like that, either. It was the thought of kissing him at all. Ever."

"Oh." Margaret chewed her pizza.

"You're looking at me funny."

"Well, usually, when I can't tolerate a man kissing me, especially if I like him and he's nice-looking, it's because I'm madly in love with somebody else. There's this built-in monogamous urge."

"I guess that's my problem, too." Adrienne didn't feel like eating anymore. She shoved the rest of the pizza toward Margaret, who was always hungry.

"You admit that you're madly in love with this guy you spent the wild weekend with? This inappropriate fly-boy?"

Adrienne nodded. "Guess I am."

"What are you going to do about it?"

"Nothing. I'll get over him. Simple as that."

GETTING OVER MATT wasn't simple, but Adrienne hadn't really believed it would be. She would do it, though. She wouldn't be like her sisters. She wouldn't allow herself the luxury of marrying someone in the name of an unpredictable emotion like love, an emotion that blinded you to the realities of life.

Adrienne's first hurdle was arranging to mail Dorothy's clothes back to Archie. Not trusting herself to speak directly to Archie, she called Mrs. Potter at the bed-and-breakfast and asked if a package addressed to Archie with only the town's name on it would reach him. Mrs. Potter assured her it would. Then before Adrienne could hang up, Mrs. Potter gave her a full report on Archie and Matt, who were involved in a big salvage operation that had captured the interest of the entire town.

Adrienne got off the line as soon as possible, packed up the freshly washed clothes and Dorothy's moccasins, and wrote a short note to Archie thanking him for the loan of the clothes. She mentioned that she was very busy at work, but perhaps in a few months she'd visit him.

She intended to do just that, but she wanted to wait until she didn't hurt quite as much, and until the excitement over the recovery of Matt's plane had died down. She thought that with luck she could maintain a friendship with Archie despite her rift with Matt. She loved the old man too much to cut him out of her life.

He'd be disappointed about the breakup, but she thought he'd want to see her again, anyway.

Her second problem came a week later when Archie wrote back to her, his letter full of misspellings and grammatical errors. He obviously wasn't used to writing, but he'd painstakingly made the effort. First he described the salvaging of the plane, but then he approached the real reason he'd written. He wanted to know what the trouble was with Matt. He said Matt was "ornery and sad-lookin' as a whipped pup." Adrienne didn't answer the letter, but she couldn't make herself throw it away, either. She tucked it in the bottom of a bureau drawer.

After that, there were no more reminders. Her life settled into its predictable routine, except for the inevitable strain that ensued whenever she encountered Alex at the office. She put in the usual grueling hours in the bull pen, the brokers' nickname for a set of six modular cubicles in the center of the offices of C. D. Girard and Sons. Rookie brokers in the bull-pen were expected to make no less than fifty telephone solicitations a day. Once every six weeks each had a turn as the floor broker, and all walk-in business belonged to whoever was in charge of the floor for the week.

Other than Sharon, the receptionist, Adrienne was the only woman in the building. Alex was one of a privileged few brokers who'd earned a private office with a window looking onto the purple-and-gray flanks of the Santa Catalina Mountains.

Word had spread quickly that Adrienne and Alex were no longer together. Most of the men closed ranks against her, blaming her, and rightly so, she thought, for the split. Kidding that had always been softened by Alex's presence became more barbed. Then two of the single brokers dropped their subtle and not-so-subtle hints that they were available. When she gave them no encouragement, they became slightly hostile.

Despite the strained working environment, Adrienne still found the work challenging, and she threw herself into it as both escape and therapy. Instead of fifty phone calls a day she tried for a hundred. She came in early and stayed late, packed her lunch and ate at her desk. She never missed being there for the closing of the market at two o'clock Arizona time—four o'clock on Wall Street.

The strenuous pace began to pay off, although Adrienne knew she lost potential clients, promising ones, who preferred to hear a man's voice advising them about stocks and bonds. She developed a thick skin about this sexist attitude and focused on the accounts she won.

She would make it; she knew that now. She worked with a greater confidence than ever. The weekend with Matt had given her a stronger self-image, she admitted. After having conquered obstacles that had appeared one after the other during those two days, making one hundred phone calls to strangers was a piece of cake. And, after having tried to predict what disaster would befall them next during that harrowing weekend, Adrienne found predicting the rise and fall of the market commonplace. Almost—she hated to say it—boring.

Arriving at the conclusion that she was bored didn't come easily to Adrienne. She skated around the revelation for a long time, refusing to acknowledge that her life was too predictable, too safe, too sane. Yet one morning before work she found herself reading a newspaper account of a skydiver and wondering if she should sign up for lessons. Then a client told her about a white-water rafting trip he'd taken and she asked for the name of the company that offered it.

But when she imagined taking the skydiving lessons or the rafting trip, Matt's face always became part of the picture. Danger and risk weren't all she craved. They were a disguise for getting close to the feelings she'd had with Matt, the excitement, the fun...and the love. A disguise, and a poor one, for getting close to Matt. She tore up the information on skydiving and rafting. She'd have to hope the effect of falling in love with Matt would eventually wear off like a coat of fingernail polish or a summer tan.

Work remained her only distraction as she trudged through November. She'd promised herself a trip home to Utah for Thanksgiving, right after the production period for November ended. Adrienne was on track for the best month of her career with a chance of surpassing all the other new brokers and a few of the established ones as well. After the way most of them had been treating her recently, she wanted that victory.

To increase her chances, she'd pulled floor duty the week of Thanksgiving. Monday and Tuesday had brought her three new clients, and all she needed was a good Wednesday and she'd have her goal pegged.

On Wednesday walk-in business was slow, but she worked doggedly on the telephone. The people she reached at home berated her for calling while they were making pumpkin pies or chopping celery for dressing. Calls to office workers weren't much better. Nobody wanted to talk about investments and a few hung up as she explained her business. She slumped in her chair, but she straightened immediately when one of the other new brokers wandered by with lifted eyebrows and a smug expression on his face.

"Bad morning, Burnham?" he asked with ill-disguised relish.

"Lovely morning, Thorndyke." She smiled. "How about you?"

"Couldn't be better," he said, and returned to his cubicle with his cup of coffee. Overhearing his next few calls gave her a small sense of satisfaction that Ted Thorndyke wasn't faring any better than she was.

At noon Adrienne opened the bottom drawer of her desk and took out her lunch sack. She always ate a sensible lunch—a salad in a Tupperware container, whole wheat crackers, and milk in a Thermos she'd bought for the purpose. She opened the plastic container and sprinkled some vinegar over the salad. She picked up her fork, stared at the salad and put her fork down again.

She couldn't eat another lunch like this one. She was tired of this lunch, this same old healthy lunch, day after day. Maybe all she needed was a vacation, she thought, covering the salad and returning her lunch sack to the drawer. She'd leave after the market closed and drive straight through to Utah, arriving in the early hours of Thanksgiving morning.

She could almost taste the trip. On the way back maybe she'd stop at Saddlehorn. Maybe she'd ride Dorothy's bike out to the canyon. Maybe she'd—

"Daydreaming, Burnham?"

Adrienne jerked back to awareness.

The assistant manager stood at her desk frowning. "I would have thought you'd be dialing that telephone," he said, adjusting his tie. "I wouldn't have thought you'd be letting down now, when you could beat some of the big boys this month. Or were you dreaming up your menu for tomorrow?"

Adrienne gritted her teeth. "I'm afraid I'm not much of a cook, Mr. Dannenger," she said. "I'm going up to Utah for Thanksgiving."

"Ah, yes. To see your parents. Have you told them how well you're doing?"

"I thought I'd see how this month finishes up before I start bragging."

"Prudent," Dannenger said with a smirk. "Very prudent."

"So if you don't mind, I will get back to my calls."

"Good idea."

She picked up the receiver and glanced at her list of names. She didn't want to call even one more person. Worst of all, she didn't even care anymore whether she broke production records this month. Dannenger lingered in the doorway of her cubicle. She smiled up at him, but as soon as he walked away she stuck her tongue out in his direction.

A familiar chuckle greeted her gesture. *Matt.* She whirled in her desk chair, and there he was, his chin in his hands as he leaned his elbows on the low wall surrounding her area. A rush of delight pushed her out of the chair. "Matt, how—" She recovered herself. The last words they'd spoken to each other hadn't been friendly. She shouldn't be glad to see him. But she was. So glad that she began to shake. "What—that is, Sharon didn't tell me that—you took me by surprise."

Matt straightened and walked to the opening in the cubicle. "I convinced Sharon that we were old friends and that it would be pompous to have you paged to come up and fetch me."

"*Fetch?* You sound like Archie." But he looked like heaven itself, she thought, savoring every sexy inch of the picture he made in his brown leather bomber jacket and tan corduroy slacks.

"I probably do sound like Archie. I've spent a lot of time with him in the past few weeks."

"I see." Adrienne remained standing, not knowing how to proceed. She wanted him to stay, at least for a few moments. His electric presence and the laughter hiding in his hazel eyes were a tonic she'd long been without. "Would you like to sit down?" she asked, indicating one of two armchairs opposite her desk.

"No, thanks. I wondered if you'd like to go to lunch."

"Lunch?" She thought of Dannenger's frown. She had floor duty, which she'd have to relinquish to someone else. That didn't show much discipline. Besides, today was the last chance she'd have to increase her sales for the production period. She'd lose at least an hour of calling.

She hesitated a moment longer. "I'd love to," she said, and experienced a rush of the emotion she'd always associate with Matt—excitement.

Unhooking her coat from a rack in the corner and taking her purse from the middle desk drawer, she walked to the partition separating her from Ted. "Thorndyke?" she called, peering over the wall.

He stood up immediately and she knew he'd been listening to every word she and Matt had said. "What?"

"How about taking floor duty for a while? I'm going to lunch."

He looked at her as if she'd grown bean sprouts for hair. "You're giving me floor duty so you can go to lunch? On the last day of the production period?"

Adrienne stared back. "Yes. Want the duty?"

"Only if you give me the rest of the day. I don't want some potential client showing up just as you walk back in, after I've been sitting here twiddling my thumbs through the lunch hour."

"All right, the rest of the day, then. I'll tell Sharon."

"Yeah. Okay." He shook his head. "I still can't believe you're going to lunch. You never go to lunch."

"Maybe I'm turning over a new leaf," Adrienne said, and walked out of the cubicle to join Matt. She took a deep breath, which gave her a good strong dose of the rustic scent of his leather jacket and the tang of his after-shave.

"You *never* go to lunch?" Matt asked, glancing at her.

"Don't start," she said. "Let's just be nice, okay? Surely we can have a civilized lunch without arguing?"

"Who's arguing?"

"I know what you were leading up to. You were about to lecture me about not having any fun, about not taking time out for lunch."

Matt chuckled again. "Maybe if you took time for lunch you wouldn't have to make faces at your boss."

"You don't know what you're talking about," she said, coloring and hoping that Sharon hadn't heard his remark.

Sharon was observing them with a smile of speculation as they approached her desk.

"I've given the floor duty to Thorndyke for the rest of the day," Adrienne said.

"You have?" Sharon tried to mask her surprise but didn't succeed. "You're not coming back?"

"Oh, of course I'll be back, but Thorndyke and I agreed that giving him the rest of the day was fairer than giving him only the lunch hour."

Matt stepped to the receptionist's desk. "Suppose she didn't make it back? What would happen?"

"I *will* be back," Adrienne said before Sharon could sufficiently recover to give an answer. "I will be here when the market closes at two, as I always am."

Matt turned toward her. "Two? You have to be back by two?" He consulted his watch. "It's after twelve now."

"I have to be back before two," she said. "I have an hour, Matt."

He gazed at her and opened his mouth as if to argue, but he closed it again. "All right," he said quietly. "An hour it is."

They walked into the parking lot and she glanced around for his Corvette. Instead he took her elbow and guided her toward a white Honda four-door sedan.

"Where's your Corvette?" she asked, trying to stay calm as she experienced the warmth of his touch on her arm.

"I'm driving this now," he said.

"Oh."

He opened the passenger door and helped her in. The interior was plain, no fancy dials or gadgets. Matt got behind the wheel and smiled at her. "Like it?"

What's to like? she thought. The car was fine, fine for someone else. It didn't suit Matt at all. "I'm sure it gets great gas mileage," she said.

"Great gas mileage," he repeated, nodding.

"The color's practical, too." She wondered why she felt so disappointed in the car. Matt had made a sensible choice in trading in the Corvette, the sort of choice she would have advised him to make if she was his financial counselor. The sort of choice she'd expect him to fight.

Matt drove the car at exactly the speed limit, no faster or slower. He didn't try to make conversation.

"How's Archie?" she asked at last.

"Fine. Sends his regards."

"Oh. Then he knew you'd be seeing me?"

"Yes."

If she'd ever dreamed Matt Kirkland would come back into her life, it wouldn't have been like this. From past experience she would have expected him to dash in and sweep her off her feet. In fact, when she'd seen him in his leather bomber jacket, she'd expected just that. Perhaps he was taking her someplace wildly exciting for lunch, and he planned to surprise her.

Instead, they pulled into Denny's. "How's this?" he asked, turning to her.

"F-fine," she stammered. "The prices are quite moderate."

"Exactly," he said. "I checked."

"You checked?"

"Sure. Didn't want to blow the budget."

"Budget?"

He smiled at her again, that bland, not-quite-like-the-old-Matt smile. "Budget," he repeated. "We're repeating ourselves, Burnham, and the conversation is beginning to sound like a passage in a first-grade reader. Shall we go in?"

She nodded, completely confused. She remembered science fiction movies in which an alien invaded the body of an earthling and transformed his personality. Something about this new Matt had that same quality.

Inside the restaurant they were seated in a booth and handed menus. Adrienne ordered a hamburger with all the trimmings; Matt ordered a tuna salad. It was as if they'd changed places. She thought perhaps he'd suggest wine. Denny's had a liquor license. He didn't, and she ordered coffee. So did he. Decaffeinated.

"All right," she said at last. "Why did you come to my office today?"

He looked at her, his eyes hooded. "To do some business."

Hope that he had some romantic scheme in mind died with that unemotional statement. But if he could pretend they'd been nothing to each other, so could she. "What kind of business?" she asked.

"I've taken your advice and sold the plane to someone who could afford to repair and insure it."

She wanted to scream at him. *Now* he'd decided to do that. Now, when it was too late, when he'd obviously lost all feeling for her. She clenched her napkin in her lap but forced herself to remain outwardly calm. "I see."

"Therefore I have some money to invest. So does Archie, as a matter of fact. We'd both like you to handle the details for us."

"Why me?"

He regarded her steadily. "We're both sure you're very good at what you do."

She had an urge to laugh. She'd imagined going out to lunch with Matt as some wild and crazy departure from routine, and yet here she was handling business whether she wanted to or not. Apparently wild and crazy wasn't in her future anymore. "What sort of investment did you have in mind?" she asked, doing her job even though she wanted to run out of the restaurant.

"Something tax-deferred, I think and not too risky. I don't care if the interest is huge, just so I'm guaranteed the money's safe."

"What?" She stared at him in disbelief.

"You heard me. I'm sure you have those kind of investments. I suspect you even specialize in them."

It was true; she did. She wished she could deny it, though, on this one occasion.

"So can you find a safe place for the money?" Matt asked.

"I guess I can," she said without enthusiasm.

"Good. Remember, low risk."

She couldn't stand it any longer. "What has happened to you, Matt Kirkland?" she exploded. "The man I used to know would have asked me for the highest yield, the up-and-coming, chancy stuff that's exciting but scary. Who's this person worried about safety?"

"Maybe it's time I tried the slow and steady approach for a while. I've been thinking of increasing my life insurance, too, and taking a second job. There's an opening in one of the malls for a shoe salesman, and I may apply for that. The pay's steady, and—"

"You're out of your mind!"

"What's wrong?"

"Don't you dare work in a shoe store! Don't you dare do it! I don't know what's gotten into you, with this tax-deferred investing, and driving that little Honda, and applying for a shoe salesman's job, but you sound ridiculous. Picturing you selling shoes is like imagining a tiger practicing needlepoint."

He looked hurt. "I thought . . . I thought you'd approve."

Adrienne looked down and toyed with her silverware. She was totally confused by her response to his plans. After all, a while ago she had advised him to move in this direction. But she'd had no idea then how she'd feel watching the old Matt slip away.

"Isn't this the sort of thing you were talking about before?" he prompted.

"Well, maybe some of your decisions are reasonable," she said, not looking at him. "Selling the plane and investing the money left over makes sense, but you seem to have lost all your—"

"Car's on fire!" shouted a man who burst through the double doors leading into the restaurant. "A red Corvette's in the parking lot and it's on fire! Anybody in here drive a red Corvette?"

"Damn!" Matt leaped to his feet. "That's gotta be mine," he muttered, and bolted out the door.

14

"YOUR CAR?" Adrienne cried, throwing down her napkin and leaping up. "But you have a white Honda!" Before she got to the door a blond man about Matt's age pushed ahead of her with a mumbled "excuse me." Then he ran out shouting Matt's name.

Adrienne followed him, and several of the restaurant patrons followed Adrienne, so that she found herself at the head of a small crowd hurrying around to the restaurant's side parking lot. A siren sounded in the distance and she could smell smoke.

When she rounded the corner she recognized Matt's old Corvette, the hood engulfed in dark smoke and licking flames. Matt and the blond man stood a few feet away waving their hands in the air and shouting at each other as the heat blistered Matt's treasured paint job. A Rural Metro fire truck careened into the parking lot and two firemen jumped off and began spraying the car with canisters of foam.

Adrienne tried to make sense of it. Matt had two cars? And if so, why would he have both of them parked at Denny's, and who was the blond guy with him? She shivered in the cold, rubbing the goose bumps on her arms. As she stood watching the burning car she realized that the atmosphere of discomfort and disaster had a familiar feel to it. In a crazy way, she felt more at home with this pandemonium than she had with the boring little lunch she and Matt had been having.

The Rural Metro crew put the fire out. Matt and his companion talked with them for a moment before the truck rumbled out of the parking lot. The restaurant patrons drifted back inside, and soon Adrienne, Matt and the blond man were the only ones left in the parking lot.

She walked over to them, hugging herself against the cold. "I don't understand," she said, her teeth chattering.

"It wasn't supposed to catch fire," Matt said, staring at the blackened car.

"It wasn't my fault, Matt," the blond man said. "Must have been some sort of electrical thing that came up all of a sudden."

"Yeah." Matt sighed.

"Honest to God, it was okay when I locked it up and went into the restaurant."

"I'm sure it was, Jack." Matt put a hand on his shoulder. "Sorry if I blew up. I've been on a short fuse lately."

Adrienne glanced from one man to the other. They seemed to be completely unaware of her. "Hello," she said, sticking out her hand toward the blond man. "I'm Adrienne."

He shook her hand. "I know."

Adrienne began losing patience. "I'm glad you're so well-informed. Everybody seems to know what's going on here except me."

Matt glanced at her. "Oh, Adrienne, meet Jack Booth."

Adrienne nodded toward Jack. "You bought Matt's car?"

"No," Jack said. "Matt borrowed my car, the white Honda. I drove his Corvette over here so that he'd have it, except now it won't run, so I guess we have one car between us," he added, turning to Matt. "Maybe I could drop you somewhere, you and Adrienne, if you—"

"Stop!" Adrienne interrupted. "None of this is adding up. Would one of you please tell me what the hell is going on around here?"

Jack shot a furtive look at Matt. "You know, I left a cup of coffee and a piece of pie in there. Maybe I'll just toddle on back and finish it, while you two work this out."

Matt grinned. "You're a coward, Jack."

"You're the one who told me she was a spitfire."

Adrienne whirled on Matt. "You said *what?*"

"See you guys," Jack said, backing away.

"Why did you tell your friend something like that about me?" Adrienne shouted.

Matt crossed his arms and gazed at her. He seemed to be suppressing a laugh. "Gee, I don't know, Adrienne."

"And stop looking at me like that, with that superior grin on your face. I have every right to be upset, after you dragged me over here in a borrowed car, for who knows what reason, and—"

"Dragged? You could hardly wait to get out of that office and away from that old mashed-potato face of a supervisor. You looked at me the way a cat looks at a dish of cream."

"I did not! I merely—"

"Come here," he said, hauling her into his arms. "That's better. Feels like old times, doesn't it, fighting like this?"

"Bad old times," she said, trying halfheartedly to struggle away. He felt so good pressed against her. Her squirming somehow only managed to fit them closer together.

"I don't think they were so bad." He rubbed the small of her back and gazed into her eyes. "That weekend was the best time of my life."

"It was absolutely insane," she said, her heart pounding as his body warmed hers.

"And wonderful."

"Impetuous."

"Yeah." He cupped her bottom and brought her in close. "You said you didn't like that sort of thing."

"That's right. I don't."

"Liar. The light went right out of those big brown eyes the minute I started talking about safe investments. But the light's back, Adrienne. Give you a catastrophe and you're back in the race, loving every minute."

"You think I *like* this stuff? Airplanes crashing, men waving shotguns, cars burning?"

"I think you love it. You hated that act I put on with the Honda and the investment talk. Come on. Be honest."

"Wait a minute. Act?" She struggled a little, but she wasn't really committed to escaping his strong grip.

"Yeah. Like Jack said, I borrowed the car, picked the restaurant and planned a bunch of boring things to talk about, to see if you'd really like that sort of junk. If you'd enjoyed yourself, I would have been long gone. The great thing was, I could tell you didn't like me that way. You were just starting to call me on it when the car caught fire."

"You made everything up?" Warnings jangled in her head. If he still had the plane, if nothing at all had changed, then she had to keep her head, somehow. Somehow she had to forget the warm rivers of desire running through her.

"I didn't make everything up."

She relaxed a little and gave her passion some room. "What really happened?"

"I sold the plane after we pulled it out of the canyon. You gave me good advice about that. And Archie and I want to make some investments, but we need a high rate of return in as short a time as possible. We're going into business together. We're putting in a landing strip on his property so I can fly tourists up there and he'll take them prospecting."

The excitement was back in his eyes, the enjoyment of life that she'd missed, that she loved. Yet he had made some changes. She took a deep breath. "Do you . . . do you have insurance on the Corvette?"

"Yes. I hate to admit this, but a little dose of your caution has been good for me."

She relaxed a little more. "But still, Matt, you *tricked* me just now," she protested, trying to work up some righteous indignation. "Considering how you trumped up this entire lunch date, I should—"

"You should let me kiss you. You know that's what you really want." His voice grew husky. "Adrienne, be honest. Have you ever felt for anyone what we felt for each other that weekend?"

"You mean all that frustration and anger? No, never."

"And all that laughter, and passion, and...and love?"

She gazed at him. No, she'd never felt that kind of love before. She felt it still.

"We taught each other how to love during that weekend," he said, "and I can't unlearn it. I need you, and I'm foolish enough to think you need me, too."

"Matt, I don't know. We're so different."

"That's what makes it fun. But we're alike in the ways that count. We both have courage, and loyalty. We both like being where the action is, although you didn't know that before. Haven't you been just a little bored without me?"

"Just a little," she admitted.

He chuckled. "More than a little?"

"All right, a lot, but—"

"That's all I need to know. Listen, I reserved a room at the Sheraton. I've ordered rose-covered sheets put on the bed. Come there with me. Now."

"To a resort?"

"We have some catching up to do. I want us to be comfortable while we do it."

Heat built within her, burning away her resistance. "Matt, that's expensive and impetuous."

"Exactly. And you'll love it."

"But I have to get back to the office," she said, throwing up one last weak protest. "The market closes soon. This is the end of the production period."

His hazel eyes looked deep into hers. "You don't care about the market, or the production period. Not right this minute. You want exactly what I want."

"I don't!" she lied, knowing that she wouldn't go back to the office today, or to Utah, either. "I...don't," she said more softly as he lowered his head and brushed his lips against hers.

"What was that again?" he murmured.

"I do," she whispered.

"Remember those words," he said, his breath warm against her lips. "You'll be needing them again—real soon." Then he kissed her, and with a sigh she abandoned herself to a lifetime of trust, love . . . and a million sinful pleasures.

Six exciting series
for you every month...
from Harlequin

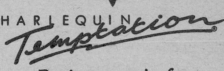
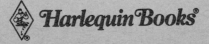